Michael C. Keith

Perspective Drifts Like a Log on a River

Michael C. Keith

Perspective Drifts Like a Log on a River

PalmArtPress
Berlin

Bibliografische Information der Deutschen Nationalbibliothek
Die Deutsche Nationalbibliothek verzeichnet diese Publikation in der Deutschen Nationalbibliografie; detaillierte bibliografische Daten sind im Internet über http://www.d-nb.de abrufbar.

ISBN: 978-3-941524-87-3

First Edition, 2017

Publisher: Catharine J. Nicely
Pfalzburger Str. 69, 10719 Berlin
Germany

www.palmartpress.com

Printed in Germany

Author's Note

This book consists of what the French call pensees—thoughts or reflections put into literary form. They are what Ray Bradbury referred to as "A particular form of writing. It's prose poetry. It's evocative. It tries to be metaphorical." I like that, because I think it comes closest to describing what exists between these covers—prose poetry that aspires to be both evocative and metaphorical.

As with my other books, this curious little volume owes much of its existence to my artist wife, Susanne Riette, who continues to understand and tolerate the behavior of the compulsive storyteller. It's not an easy row to hoe . . . just ask her.

A further note of appreciation is also owed Christopher Sterling for his steadfast commitment to pointing out my failings and for making valuable suggestions to address them.

Finally, as any writer will tell you, literary role models are vital to the process as well. So thank you, Lydia Davis and Joy Williams.

Content

Words are pain
peeled in elegant threads
like skin
torn off the body
stitched into meaning

– Christopher Reilley

Bless Me, Father, for *You* Have Sinned

I came out of the confessional booth at St. Mary's, did my Act of Contrition—six Hail Marys and five Our Fathers—and told my mom what Father Porter asked me.

"Huh . . .? Say again. What did he say, Billy?"

"If I had any sinful relations. I think he meant like, ah . . . *sex*," I replied.

"Sex? Why would he ask you such a thing? You're only 12. What do you know about sex?"

I puzzled over her question for a moment and responded, "Nothing. But it was kind of weird the way he asked it. He sounded different."

"Well, what did you say? Did you tell him you're just a child?"

"Yes," I answered, adding, "He was quiet for a while, except for some rustling sounds. Then he asked if I ever do anything sinful to myself."

My mom looked at me funny like she does when I've done something wrong. She didn't say anything else until we pulled into the driveway at home.

When we climbed from the car, she turned to me and said, "You know, Billy, sometimes I think you just like to make things up."

A Second Wind

Over the years, Jacob and Caprice Leiberman, both ornithologists, had stockpiled barbiturates to take when they became too old and infirm to enjoy life. They planned to wash down the pills with a bottle of champagne and go to sleep in each other's arms. When Caprice decided the time had arrived to execute their exit plan, her husband happened to be riding an emotional high from the kudos he was receiving for his groundbreaking research on the clade origin of the Red-breasted Coua. Given that it was the singular event of his long career, he urged his wife to go ahead without him.

On the Road . . . Again

Jack and Neal stand in the doorway of a tenement on West 113th Street. It's a chilly day but the sun is bright. Jack is lost in thought while Neal snaps his fingers and bobs to-and-fro to something only he hears.

"Dig the beat," he says.

"Beat? What beat? I don't hear any beat," scowls Jack, flipping his spent Camel into the gutter.

He looks past Neal to the dimly lit hallway where Joyce stands with her hands on her hips in a gesture of defiance.

"Fuck," mumbles Jack, as he turns and walks away.

Neal follows, be-bopping over the cracks in the cement.

Did Ted Abuse Sylvia? Rumor Is He Did

Sylvia: "Well, I like it just the way it is."

Ted: "But why ever would you use an ellipsis there?"

Sylvia: "Because nothing else would work as well."

Ted: "Those dots are such a magician's ruse."

Sylvia: "It's my poem, after all."

Ted: "Yes, it is, love. Yes, *it* is."

Sylvia: "I must get my soul back from you."

Rocky Mountain High

When we landed in Denver, "The Mile High City," we immediately found that our breathing had become somewhat labored. The next day as we drove to Breckenridge we experienced increased breathing problems, and when we finally reached Leadville, our ultimate destination, we were found asphyxiated in our rental.

The Lady Upstairs

She told me I needed to put some meat on my bones . . . that I was unhealthy skinny. Then she ran a brush through my hair flattening my pompadour. *There, you look better. That big old wave on your head just made you look like one of them Palmetto trees*, she said, patting my cheek. I liked her, but she tried to do things with the way I looked. Most of the time I didn't like what she did. Once she made me try on a shirt she said wasn't a girls, but I kind of thought it was. Another time she held some cloth against my waist for a pair of shorts she said she was going to make me because my dungarees were too hot in the Georgia summer. The only reason I visited her was for the dime she always gave me after she tried to make me look like the kid in the pictures she had all over her place.

The Xylophobe

Cy Lipton couldn't get the sound of a xylophone out of his head. It accompanied him wherever he went and served as the soundtrack for all of his dreams. Simply put, he was haunted by the instrument. Finally, he decided to see a psychiatrist. After weeks of consultations, the doctor reached a diagnosis. "Mr. Lipton," he said, "You have a severe case of Lionel Hampton."

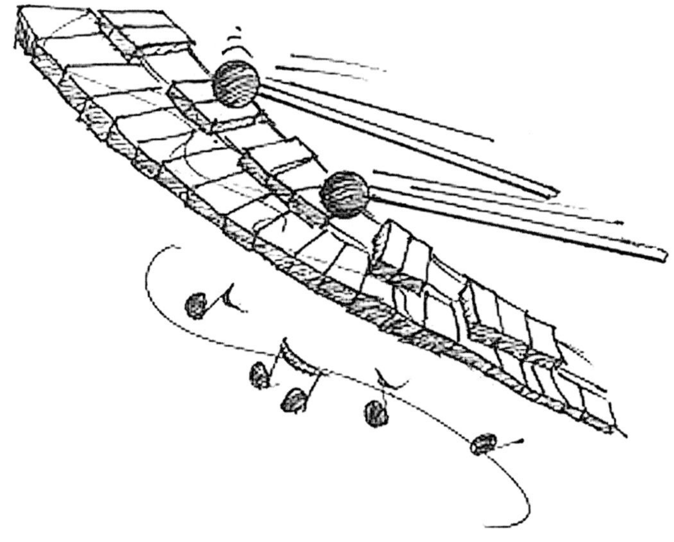

Burned out Fuselage of a Downed Aeroflat Airbus

When the Delta 737 touched down at Pulkovo Airport, Camille believed she saw the charred remains of a Stegosaurus. *It's a good thing they took care of it before it caused a problem*, she thought.

Gender Bender

He got home from work just a few minutes after his typical arrival time. As usual, supper was on the table. Tonight's repast included, fried chicken, mashed potatoes, and green peas. It was one of her favorite meals. As soon as she sat down, he entered from the kitchen with two tall iced teas and welcomed her home. She said hello and dove into the spread before him. Following supper, she cleared the table, and he headed to his job at the oil refinery where she had worked for nearly a decade. "Be safe," he shouted from the kitchen, as he filled the dishwasher. "I will," she answered, and drove to the mall to pick up a wrench set at Sears. He quickly purchased what he needed and drove back home. After watching TV's "Who Do You Think You Are?" they turned in for the night, he on one side of the bed and she on his side. The next morning, she arrived back home from her overnight shift at the Seven-Eleven exhausted and ready to hit the sack until noon when he had to go to the gynecologist for his annual checkup. Immediately following her appointment, he returned home and accused her of acting like another person over the last few days. "Oh!" she responded, in a deep muscular tone, "And I suppose you think you're the perfect *woman*, Mister?"

At the Hogwarts School, a Question Was Posed

Over one hundred books have been written about Big Foot. Can something be studied so extensively and not exist?

The Lord Shows Early Signs of Practicing What He Will Preach

According to the Gospel, Jesus had a fairly normal childhood. Joseph and Mary knew he was bright and gave him more freedom than most parents. As a youngster of 10, he had a number of friends and played the popular games of the day. War games were among the favorites of boys, who would make wooden swords and engage in mock battles. On one such occasion, Jesus jousted with Jaakobah, beating him decisively—first disarming him and then whacking him across his knee. The defeated youngster began to cry as onlookers chided Jesus for his ill deed. After a moment, the future Savior spoke up, saying he was not feeling himself and asked for forgiveness. Jaakobah replied that he would forgive Jesus if he could hit him in the knee with his sword. Jesus thought about it for a moment and then declared that he could not condone an act of revenge.

A Common Theme

When I read of stable, normal childhoods, I wait for the boom to drop . . . the father coming home drunk and beating his wife . . . the mother suddenly terminally ill . . . siblings getting in trouble with the law. Memoirs are made of this stuff. It's good for them that things turn to shit. Who wants to read about a life free of conflict?

Hearing Problems

She was angry about something I said today. Yesterday I said something that set her off. And the day before that she was unhappy with something else I said. Tomorrow I'll seek shelter as far away from the reach of her ears as possible, because her aural perception of me is clearly *un*sound.

eMotion

We walk but don’t want to be walking. We both feel we should, but we’d prefer just staying in our air-conditioned apartment with our iPads, iPods, and iPhones. We figure two miles is how far we need to walk to gain anything from being out walking. About a quarter of a mile into our walk, we’ve lost interest.

“Let’s go back,” she says.

And I say, “Yeah, let’s go back. Walking is just so tedious. Why do people do it?” I ask.

She says, “Because they say it’s good for you.”

I ask, “Who says that walking is good for you?”

And she says, “I don’t know . . . someone on the Internet, I think.”

The Depths of Reason

My dad says his cousin, my second cousin, appeared in "20,000 Leagues Under The Sea." I ask what's happened to him, thinking we might get in touch with him in Hollywood, since I'm an aspiring movie star. My dad answers that the giant squid-like monster in the movie ate the diving bell that his actor-cousin was descending in, so communicating with him is impossible.

Perspective Drifts Like a Log on a River

Dan Simmons sat on his backyard patio gazing at the snow-capped mountains in the distance. He reflected back on the long and bumpy road that had led him to where he now was at 59 years old. His young adult life had gotten off to a rough start with the death of his parents within three months of each other. It had forced him to drop out of college because of a lack of funds (he'd discovered his father had lost everything in an ill-conceived business venture just before his fatal car accident) and take a series of menial jobs while attending classes at night. Six years later he'd finally obtained his undergraduate degree and after three more years his masters. While in graduate school he'd met a fellow student with whom he shared many things in common, in particular an abiding affection for drugs. They were soon living together and not long after married. By their tenth anniversary, the union had fallen apart for a raft of reasons and Dan found himself living alone in a small central Pennsylvania town where he taught English and history at the middle school. He'd always been drawn to the west, in particular New Mexico, and after a decade of a solitary, if not monastic, existence, he decided to apply for teaching jobs in the so-called Land of Enchantment.

To his satisfaction, his first round of applications resulted in two job offers, and he decided on one at a small, prestigious private high school just outside of Santa Fe. It was no more that two months into the first semester at the school that he met and fell in love with another teacher nearly two decades his junior. In the coming years, he settled into a bucolic existence with his new mate and their two children, who—along with his wife—were the love of his life. Now, lounging in his yard as the sun slipped over the Rockies, he realized that things were not as perfect as he had felt, because he was plagued by a deep feeling of remorse. He could not shake the thought that he had foolishly opted for a domestic SUV rather than a more fuel-efficient foreign model.

Tell Me about It

People come into the bar to see Sully. He makes you feel welcome, and he's never stingy with the booze. He's also a great listener. My girlfriend says that's because he has three ears. I say he'd be a great listener even if he only had two.

Careful What You Wish For

Marge worked as the assistant manager at a souvenir store on the Taos Plaza. Her principal duty involved manning the store's cash register. It was not her favorite task but one she spent most of her day doing. Consequently over time she developed a keen dislike for both her customers and the products she sold. *If I have to deal with one more person asking about a stupid Kokopelli, please shoot me in the frigging head.* As fate would have it, one afternoon she spotted a young man slip one of the shop's pricier items—a *Kokopelli* that actually was what it claimed to be: an original Native American work—into his shirt. As the would-be thief headed for the door, Marge grabbed him. At that moment, the assailant drew a gun and shot her dead. When the sheriff questioned the young man, who happened to be of Indigenous descent, as to why he killed the store employee for a piece of cheap statuary, the youth answered, "This ain't no phony *Kokopelli*. This one makes wishes come true."

Silent Migraines

After examining my eyes, the ophthalmologist said, "I have bad news and good news. The bad news is you are suffering from what we call silent migraines. The good news is that you don't experience the painful headaches that accompany regular migraines, but you will have occasions when you will not fully see what is in front of you."

Unsolved Mystery

Angie bought a used story collection by Lorrie Moore on Amazon. It came pretty tattered but still intact enough to read. She considered complaining but then figured for $2.00 it was acceptable in the shape it was in. As she was thumbing through its dog-eared pages for a title that might engage her, an index card fell out. It contained one ink scrawled sentence that aroused her curiosity. “Would you do it for me?” it read. *What was it that its writer wanted done, and by whom?* she puzzled, further speculating that it might possess some nefarious intent. *Harm someone, commit a robbery, set fire to a building. . .?* She thought about it for a while longer and then decided to use the card as a bookmark.

Visionary

She sat down on the cold cement and stared at the wall. No one knew what she was seeing, and the small crowd that had gathered out of curiosity figured the woman was mentally challenged. After a couple of minutes the group began to disburse but stopped when the woman began to laugh hysterically. Laughter being contagious, several people joined in. Soon the woman stood up and faced her audience, giving the assemblage a quizzical look. "So, you guys think blank walls are funny, too . . . *really*?" she said, and walked away.

Making Unnecessary Life Adjustments

She woke up dying following a dream about her mother's fatal car accident. Moments after her alarm clock sounded, she felt a sharp pain in her chest and knew the end was upon her. The doctors had said she was a prime candidate for sudden cardiac arrest and here it was. No big surprise, she thought, accepting that it was her time to go just as it had been her mother's time. *You can't drive as recklessly as your mother does and not get in a bad accident*, her father had said. She had always been very careful behind the wheel not wanting to replicate her mother's fate.

Everything Is Food to Something

Marvin was boiling eggs and thinking: *Is this right? These things were going to have a life, and here I am about to make egg salad out of them for lunch. Maybe that's what cancer is all about . . . making us into a meal.*

Hypergraphiacosis

I told my friends that for years I haven't been able to stop writing. Morning, noon, and night words pour out of me. That's wonderful, they said. You must have many books to your credit by now. I said no. That, in fact, I didn't have anything that constituted a full text. They were surprised and asked why. I answered that while the words keep flowing from my brain unabated they just don't seem to be able to assemble themselves into a coherent whole.

Flights of Fancy

Err Disaster

The plane bounces hard, and I spill my Bloody Mary on my wife. She yelps and complains that I've ruined her new skirt. I apologize, and when the seat belt sign goes off, I move to a vacant seat for the rest of the flight hoping it will be less turbulent there.

* * *

Economy Class

When the flight attendant asks if I'd like a snack, I say, "Yes, may I have some caviar? She says, "Of course, sir."

* * *

Fellow Travelers

So this guy dressed in black head-to-toe sits across from me at the airport. He keeps looking at me, but I try not to look at him. After a few minutes, I can't help but give him a hard stare because he's creeping me out. When I do, he gives me a grin, and I look away again. *Screw you*, I think, and I can feel my pulse quicken.

Fag, I mumble, and I check to see if he's still got his eyes on me. He does, and I pop. "You got a problem?" I growl, and he says, "Problem? Why no. I just thought you look familiar." I figure that's bullshit and say, "Why's that?" "I'm a military chaplain, he answers, and asks if I was in Iraq. I'm surprised at this, because I was. "Yeah, I say. How'd you know?" "How couldn't I?" he replies, and looks away.

* * *

Reluctant Flyer

The Jet Blue 320A lifts from the Logan Airport tarmac and my wife squeezes my sweaty hand reassuringly. *Oh, God, God, God*! I scream in my head until the aircraft banks sharply to its left and even my thoughts are rendered speechless.

* * *

Rising to the Occasion

The passenger in front of me lowers her seat as far as it will go. I've never seen one drop back so far, and it hits my knees. When I ask if she'd mind raising it some, she says, "It's my right to lower it as much as I want." I say, "Oops, I didn't mean to spill my hot coffee on you."

Jet Lagged

The baggage carousel has circled many times, and I'm becoming anxious about loosing my suitcase. *Shit, did it end up on another flight to God only knows where?* I wonder. Finally, all the luggage is gone, as are all the passengers on my former flight. *Dammit!* I grumble and look for assistance. When I locate help, I rant and rage about the incompetence of the airline, and then it occurs to me I only had a carry on.

* * *

Cabin Pressure

My bladder is about to burst, but I'm reluctant to wake the two passengers next to me. Finally, I'm force to take action and pee into my soda can. Relieved, I doze off and when the pilot announces we're about to land, I notice the can has up turned onto the passenger next to me. When he sees I'm staring at his lap, he reddens and says, "I must have wet my pants." I say nothing and give him a look of sympathy.

* * *

Flying Solo

Tracing our flight on the screen on the back of the seat in front of me is not what my wife considers the height of excitement, but she knows I'm a wannabe navigator. Today we're flying to Denver to visit our son and grandkids. As the image of our plane crosses western Kansas, I alert my wife that we'll be landing soon, but she's sound asleep. When our pilot says to prepare for landing, I try to wake her, but she doesn't respond. It takes me shaking her shoulders to realize she's unconscious . . . maybe dead. I feel a slight sense of gratification knowing that the last time we spoke was precisely over southern Wisconsin.

* * *

Sometimes You Need To Take Extreme Measures

"Every plane could be a marked plane," said Jack to his reluctant flyer friend. "You just don't know . . . there's really no guarantees. If someone wants to take it down, it's pretty damn hard to stop them."

Jack continued to rant about the chances of a mid-air terrorist attack until Larry could no longer take it. He excused himself saying he was going to the restroom one last time before takeoff. He then went to a nearby

TSA officer and reported that he'd overheard a person saying how easy it would be to blow up a plane.

"Who is this person?" asked the officer.

Larry pointed to Jack, and the airport official called for backup.

"A very scary individual," said Larry, who proceeded to the restroom as planned.

When he emerged, he joined the queue waiting to board his flight as his friend was being escorted away by security.

Note Accompanying Supper

I come home after nine hours on the assembly line. It's late and dark. My bloody arthritis is really killing me. When I enter the flat, I smell supper. I'm starving, and I shout to my wife that I'm home and ask what's for supper. She doesn't answer so I go to the kitchen. There's a plate on the table and a note next to it. It reads, "Gone out with the girls. Eat your fish sticks."

When a Friend Knows Exactly What to Say

Frank and Bernice jogged at a casual pace along Blackstone Boulevard on the East Side of Providence, Rhode Island. The longtime friends met once or twice a week for some exercise and to talk about a variety of things, mostly related to books and writing. Frank had on the windbreaker he had inherited after his father's death a month earlier. He told Bernice it was the first time he'd worn it and that it was about the only thing he had to attest to his father's former existence on the planet. Bernice knew the story of Frank's dad. He'd been a chronic alcoholic and ne'er-do-well throughout his life. At 76 he'd died of pneumonia following his latest bout with the bottle. The chronic emphysema from 60 years of a two pack a day smoking habit had so wrecked his lungs that he was unable to fight off what was a particularly nasty strain of the infection. As they continued their run, Frank suddenly let out a gasp. In the pocket of the jacket were his father's false teeth. He removed the dentures and showed them to Bernice. They both stared at the tobacco stained and chipped upper plate for a moment. Bernice then took it from Frank and with dramatic fanfare declared, "Alas, poor Yorick, we got your choppers!"

The Philosopher with a Background in Cell Biology Begins Her Lecture

"Everything in life has its limits. Take the prokaryotic cell, for instance . . . "

We All Grieve in Our Own Way

When I arrived at my mother-in-law's house, I found my wife, Suzie, and her sisters, Bella and Rose, sitting at the kitchen table attempting to deal with the fact that their grandmother had just been struck and killed by a car on 163rd Street. Less than two hours earlier they'd been given the horrible news, and in the aftermath of the tragedy they were trying to console one another with stories about their time with the 84 year-old Sicilian-immigrant they loved.

"Leave it to *Nonni* to walk to bingo instead of asking for a ride. Just like her, bad knees and all," said Bella.

"She was always so independent. That's one of the things I most admired about her," added Rose.

"I think she was getting more stubborn with age when it came to doing things herself. She just wouldn't let anyone tell her what to do or help her. The only person she ever listened to was *Nonno*," reflected my wife.

All three women sniffled and wiped tears from their bloodshot eyes.

"Can I do anything? How's your mom taking it?" I asked.

"She just went to the funeral home," answered Rose.

"We wanted to go with her, but she wouldn't let us," said Bella.

"Kind of like her mom, huh?" I ventured.

"Too bad Daddy's away. But he'll be back early tomorrow," offered Suzie.

"I just can't believe *Nonni*'s gone," mumbled Rose, suddenly smiling. "Remember when she did the boogie-woogie at your wedding? She had everyone in hysterics."

"What about the crazy hats she made," offered Suzie.

"Oh, God, the one with the tall daisy that looked like a palm tree," recalled Bella.

All three sisters broke into laughter that was short lived when Rose let out a mournful sob.

"The police said she must have just eaten pizza because it was all over her dress and on the ground where the car hit her. Mom said she had a big supper before going off to bingo, too," chuckled Bella. "Isn't that so like *Nonni*? God, she was so funny."

Why would she think that *was something to wax nostalgic about . . . her grandmother being eviscerated*, I thought, feeling nauseated by the image it conjured in my mind. Later I raised the subject with my wife, who didn't seem to understand why I thought her sister's observation peculiar.

"Well, jeez, Suzie. Think about it."

"What . . .?"

"*What*? Like the car hitting your grandmother so hard that it knocked her guts out onto the street? That was something to feel warm and fuzzy about?"

"Well, that was . . ."

"Macabre . . . *ghoulish*, maybe?"

"You just don't understand," my wife replied.

And I never did.

Audacity

Carla drew landscapes with pastels her entire life. After completing her 2,000th picture, she decided she needed a major change, so she switched to painting landscapes with acrylics.

Remains of the Day

In the late 2050s, when members of America's powerful celebrity elite finally assumed the highest posts in government, interest in viewing the corpses of long dead famous people took hold. While this raised certain ethical questions and required the permission of any existing descendants of the noted figures, it became a huge craze. At first the focus was on pop icons, like Michael Jackson and Prince, but soon the carcasses of prominent writers, artists, and politicians were exhumed for public display . . . at a price—the bigger the name the higher the fee for viewing. After a decade, the trend faded and was supplanted by an all-consuming desire to observe luminaries in their final days of a terminal illness.

Dumbest Thing Humans Say: "There Is No Intelligent Life beyond Earth."

There are 1,000,000,000,000,000,000,000,000 planets in our observable universe. Therefore, it is a reasonable assumption that life forms elsewhere can actually spell out that number.

Change of Heart

Ginsberg loves Kerouac. Has a deep thing for him. Wants desperately to bed him. He goes to Hurley's to seek him out. When he gets there, he finds Cassady with Kerouac . . . the latter half soused. The two wave to him as he enters the smoky saloon. "Where you been, man?" asks Jack. "We've been waiting here for an hour with no scratch to buy a brew. You got some dough, I hope." Ginsberg nods that he does, and Cassady flags the barkeep. "Three tall ones," he shouts, and Ginsberg says no, make his a Red Zinfandel. "You fucking fag poets!" blurts Kerouac. Ginsberg decides he no longer loves Kerouac . . . but still wants to blow him.

Last One Standing

Being alone is very difficult.

Yoko Ono

At 70 years of age Eugene Bickford wondered if he'd be the first to go. At 80 he had seen several friends and two relatives die. At 90 he was the last one left in his close circle. He was alone and felt it would have been better had he passed before everyone else had. Compounding his sense of isolation was the fact that there wasn't anyone in the elderly care center where he resided with whom he could connect in any meaningful way. A few folks were pleasant enough, but he had nothing in common with them, so essentially he kept to himself. It wasn't hard to do, since most of the center's ancient and infirm residents were confined to their beds or wheelchairs.

Eugene was among a handful that could still get around without assistance and this allowed him to stroll the facility's small but well-tended garden. It's bright flowers cheered him as much as anything could, and he figured that when he was no longer able to spend this precious time outdoors, he would hasten his end by not taking nourishment. It would be his chosen form of mercy killing, and no one could stop him since he'd specified he was not to be kept alive intravenously.

Soon the time came when he could no longer get around on his own, and he stopped eating as he had contemplated. The staffers and nurses at the elderly home did everything they could to get him to eat, but his resolve was strong and he held to his plan. In a short period of time he was not strong enough to move about freely and eventually was confined to his bed. Hoping to get him to change his mind, the caregivers brought him fresh clippings of the flowers from the garden and placed them around his room. Still he would only consume water and even this he did reluctantly. There was nothing anyone there could do and no one outside of the home who might get the nonagenarian to stop his fasting. The staff could only watch as he faded away.

Eugene's last moments were spent in reminiscences of his beloved wife when the two were young newlyweds and beginning their long, happy marriage. Although they had been childless, their lives were full of joy as they pursued their careers and mutual, as well as individual, pastimes. A passion for travel took them around the world and their separate diversions enriched their time as they each joined special interest groups and participated in activities that occasioned trips together to fun locales.

Everything considered, the Bickfords had enjoyed a bucolic existence, but the passing of Eugene's wife a decade earlier had left him feeling purposeless. His lifelong enthusiasm for nature photography dwindled, as did his fervor for trekking the globe. Nothing sustained his enthusiasm without his spouse.

Eugene finally slipped into a coma and was given the last rights. He held on for another week and then passed away. When the funeral home's hearse arrived to collect his body, Eugene found himself in the center's garden roaming the small paths between the vibrant flowerbeds. By the time his remains were driven away, he had been ushered inside an unidentifiable object that sped skyward and vanished without being detected by man or radar.

Welcome, said a voice he'd known and loved more than any in his life. *We're going on a very long and wonderful trip.*

Forewarned

There's a limb creaking on the old elm tree in front of our house. It bends toward me as I walk under it. How much more do I need to be told?

Burked*

I speak now from under the surgeon's hacksaw as he removes my cranium to access my brain. I'm an involuntary cadaver donor murdered so that a medical school can reveal the secrets of the human form to its students. They surround my lifeless body as the cutting and organ removal proceeds. Expressions of horror and awe cover their faces as I'm adeptly dismantled. Soon I'm reduced to an array of unctuous innards fondled and probed by the interns. Some of me is put into a slop bucket next to the surgery table (is it to feed the sows, I wonder?) while other pieces are wrapped and stored for later purposes. When the instructor has completed his dissection, he and his pupils leave me and the amphitheater is darkened. Some hours later the dome is relit by the hospital custodian, who then sits next to my diminished corpse and eats his kidney pie.

* "Nineteenth century practice of killing someone for the purpose of selling the body for dissection."
Oxford English Dictionary

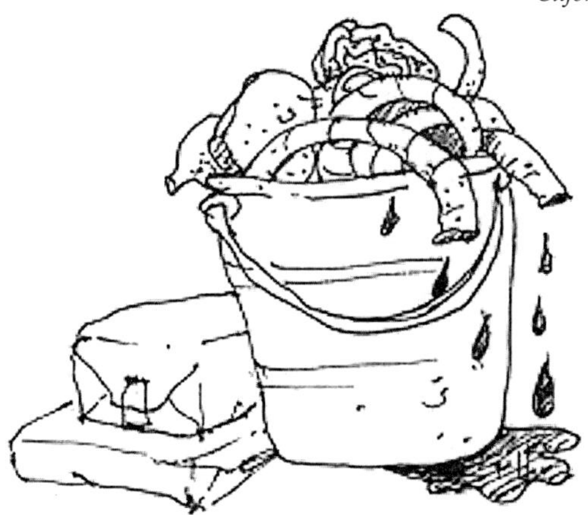

Mercy

A gathering of fellow beach goers a few hundred feet away drew Will's attention. His buddies were sound asleep as he rose and went to where the dozen or so people had congregated. An opening in the ranks of the onlookers revealed a couple of large dark objects in the sand. *Maybe seals washed ashore. No, something bigger*, he thought, and then realized they were human beings. Two large black women in bathing suits lay motionless. *Did they drown? Are they still alive? How come everybody's just standing around and doing nothing?* Will looked up and down the beach to see if any lifeguards or medics were coming but saw no such activity. There were no sirens indicating someone had called for help either. The only sounds were the waves hitting the shore and the voice of Frank Sinatra on a distant transistor radio crooning his latest hit. "What happened?" Will asked a spectator holding a small child. "I don't know," she replied nonchalantly and walked away. The unconscious women were covered with sand flies giving the impression they'd been in the same spot for a while. No other black people were on the beach. Apparently, no friends or relatives had accompanied the women, who looked like they'd simply been dumped and abandoned. As Will considered doing something because no one else was, the crowd began to disburse. In a matter of minutes, he was left alone with the bodies. *Why had no one tried to revive them? Maybe I should give them mouth-to-mouth.* He moved a couple steps toward the inert figures and then suddenly stopped and stepped back. *No . . . no way I can put my lips on theirs*, he decided, and returned to where he'd been sunning himself.

Professions with Ethics Issues

"Flowers? Don't tell me I don't like flowers. I *love* flowers. What do you think I do for a living? I sell flowers," refuted the owner of Joyful Blooms to a protestor in front of his store.

"Well, if you *loved* flowers, you wouldn't *kill* them for money," replied the horticultural activist.

Forthcoming Past

The *SS Ericsson* anchors at Pier 84 in Manhattan on the Hudson. It carries thousands of smiling and cheering troops just returned from the battlefields of Europe. It is 1946 and from where I sit gazing at this grainy photo 70 years later, it occurs to me that all of these young men so eager to get on with their lives have by now spent them.

Blank Page

Gerald urgently wanted to become a renowned writer, and he took serious steps to help realize his goal. He enrolled in the best writing program and apprenticed with two prominent authors. By the time he was set to launch his own career, he found he had writer's block. Desperate to unlock his muse, he enlisted in the army for a tour of duty in the war zones of the Mideast. Still suffering from his creative impasse upon discharge, he joined a friend in an attempt to circumnavigate the globe in a kayak. It took two years and in the process his companion fell gravely ill forcing Gerald to complete the voyage alone. When he returned to where the daring venture had begun, he immediately signed up for Sherpa training in the Himalayans. Four more years of intrepid activities followed, but the fiction he dreamed of producing continued to elude him. On his fortieth birthday, he became a smokejumper in the High Sierras and later a logger in the Yukon. More years of perilous undertakings ensued and finally Gerald gave up on the idea of becoming a noted author, concluding that he just didn't have any material from which he could draw inspiration.

When You Want What You Want and Will Go to Any Length to Get It

Lydia wanted Lucky Charms desperately. *I'd kill for a bowl*, she thought, as she calculated how long it would take her to get to the 7-Eleven. In ten minutes she was scouring the shelves of the convenient store for her favorite sugary fix but couldn't find it. At first police were baffled as to the motive behind the killing of the store clerk and the apparent suicide of his assailant until an officer discovered the store was out of the cereal.

Duel Purpose

Two friends of Leon's were in the end stages of their individual maladies, and he felt he'd be called upon to give eulogies for both men sooner than later. Anticipating this, he went through his closet looking for something appropriate to wear at these austere events. He'd given up wearing suits following his retirement a dozen years earlier, relying on sport jackets and slacks for occasions that required a level of dress up. After a few minutes, he determined that the outfits that still hung in his wardrobe were too casual for a funeral. He was surprised by his former predilection for odd colors. *Did I really wear those?* When he complained about this to his wife, she reminded him that all he needed was a basic black suit.

"Suits aren't cheap, you know. And considering how often I'll wear one . . . "

"Well, think of it this way, you'll get multiple uses out of it," she offered.

"How so?" he asked.

"You can wear it to funerals, and I can dress you in it for your own."

Ugly American

He whistled unconsciously as he descended the narrow wooden stairs inside the onion domes of St Basil's. An attendant who reminded him of Nikita Khrushchev gave him an admonishing look. "Nyet," she growled, holding her thick finger over her lips.

A Friend to the End

For several years, Miguel had dreaded mandatory retirement and he made his concern well known to his closest friend, Felipe. He was okay financially, but he just didn't have a clue what to do when his career was over. The idea of endless time with nothing specific to do depressed him. Finally, it was Felipe who came up with a solution.

"You've always said you'd rather die than retire. Am I right, amigo?" he asked, clutching a brown bag in his hand.

"Yeah, I have. Can't deal with the idea of it, man," replied Miguel.

"Well, *mi hernando*, I hate to see you like this. So I've given this a lot of thought and think I've come up with an answer," said Felipe . . . handing his friend what he'd been holding.

"*What the* . . . ?" blurted Felipe, removing a gun from the sack.

"Yeah, I know, Miguel," said Felipe, smiling warmly. "You'd do the same for me . . . *no*?"

Book Worm

My friend really doesn't read books. He just wants people to think that. What he actually does is buy tomes with pithy titles to dazzle people with his sophistication. He then asks if they'd like to read them when he's done. If they say yes—and they usually do, because they want to look smart, too—he goes through the books and dog-ears them at 100 page intervals to give the impression he's read them with sustained interest.

The Shill

An elderly Chinese man poured coins into the dollar slot machine night after night. Burt watched from his perch above the floor of the casino from where he enticed customers to spend more money during what was called Double Jackpot Time—"Hey, folks, for the next 60 seconds, if you hit a jackpot, it's worth double the amount . . . " He calculated the old man put several hundred dollars an evening into the one armed bandit, and when Burt launched into his spiel, the diminutive player accelerated his efforts. *Jesus, he must be rolling in dough to be doing that*, thought Burt. After a couple of weeks watching the unlucky gambler, he was actually relieved when he finally hit a jackpot. The man whooped and shouted as the machine blinked and rang in defeat. *Well, it's about time*, thought Burt, and then he realized the payout was only $200. *Damn, the guy must have dumped $20 grand to get a fraction of it back, and he's acting like he's brought the house to its knees.* After his shift, Burt saw the senior high roller leaving the casino and decided to ask him why he was so ecstatic about winning an amount that was so insignificant compared to what he'd lost. "Well, young man," he answered, "As Confucius say, 'He who lusts only after riches, fails to see life's truly valuable things.' Besides," he added, smiling slyly "I own the casino."

Some Will Benefit from His Decision and Some Will Not

The AR-15 cost more than he had. The only gun he could afford was a low caliber pistol, so he decided to wait until he had enough money to do the job right.

Upon Witnessing a Dialogue between Aliens

"Your color sense is truly unique," said Celia, one half of the new couple we'd recently met.

This was the first time they'd been over so we were keen to hear their impressions of our house.

Thanks," said my wife, Sheri, who was an artist and accustomed to getting raves for her decorative choices.

"You really love primary colors, don't you?" asked Celia.

"Not really," replied my wife.

I could tell she was a bit put off by Celia's comment.

"Mostly I like soft tones. Occasionally, bright reds and blues mix well with less assertive hues."

"Like in this room, right? It's loud, but it works really well."

"Oh, I wouldn't call it *loud*. Perhaps you mean *engaging*?"

"Oops, I meant loud in a *good* way."

"I always interpret loud as meaning garish or tawdry?"

"Sorry, maybe I'm using the wrong term. How about showy? No, ornate. Yes, that's it . . . *ornate.*"

"To me that suggests pretentious or glitzy. I wouldn't call this room's color scheme ornate."

"Oops, my bad. Guess they just aren't the shades I'd have in my home, but you're the artist and know more about that than I do."

"Speaking of which, I love your skirt, but I think it clashes with your blouse," said Sheri, her right eyebrow arched critically. "You really shouldn't attempt to blend patterns like that. They also add weight to your appearance."

At that point, I suggested that Celia's husband, Burt, join me on the patio figuring the doors to hell were about to open and suck us in. Once safely beyond the growing verbal pyrotechnics of our wives, we drank a beer and exchanged small talk that soon led to a deeper discussion about the local sports teams.

A half-an-hour had passed and I wondered if blood had been spilled between Sheri and Celia when they emerged from the house arm-and-arm as if they were the best of friends.

“What happened?” I asked, unable to contain my curiosity. “We thought . . . ”

“*Thought* what?” my wife shot back, shrugging her shoulders and smiling at Celia. “Try to understand men, if you can.”

The Importance of Quality Sound

Sotheby's was engaged in a debate about an item called Hiroshima Glass. According to its owner, the artifact came from ground zero of the bombing of the Japanese city. What he claimed made it unique—beyond it having survived the atomic blast—was that it contained the residue of victims of the detonation. When he told Sotheby's that one could actually hear the casualties' final agonized gasps if one put one's ear close to it, the auction house decided to end its representation of the object on the basis that the intonations were analog rather than digital, which it believed significantly reduced its monetary value.

Vindication?

After several years, the writer completed her critical, if not condemning, satire of the book industry only to have it enthusiastically accepted by one if its largest presses. She couldn't decide whether to be happy or pissed. *Did I spend all this time in vain*? she wondered.

Short Attention Span

A line of flashing blue lights along the Providence River caught Gower's attention as he stood on the terrace of his high-rise. The first thing that entered his mind was that they must be looking for a body or had found one. The local crime syndicate was famous for disposing bodies in the murky waterway that snaked through the city. Distant sirens grew louder and then their source appeared. Two ambulances joined the string of cop cars. *Must be more than one victim*, thought Gower, noticing television vans with their satellite dishes raised. *Hm, they're probably sending live feeds from there? Let me check.* He went inside and turned on his 60" LG flat screen. The first thing that appeared was "Sponge Bob Square Pants" on the Cartoon Channel. *God, that Squidward Tentacles character knocks me out*, muttered Gower, totally engrossed.

Sometimes a Brilliant Notion

Doing things you think are smart are frequently stupid.
But doing nothing is almost always stupid.
Curtis B. Michaels

Since he'd moved to St. Louis from rural Menfro, Missouri, Cal Hedlong had found it nearly impossible to get to sleep. The electric street lights that had been installed just weeks before he took up residence in a modest, second floor flat on Drury Street had kept him awake no matter what he did to dull them. The clanking noise from the passing horse-drawn trollies impaired his ability to doze off as well. In desperation, he had placed a heavy wool blanket over the dwelling's only window to muffle the racket and block the outside glare, but both still managed to seep in.

Cal had come to the metropolis in search of something other than farm work and in the hope of finding a lady friend more appealing than the handful of women his age back home. The tiny river town he'd left afforded him little opportunity in either area. However, after a year of unsatisfying jobs and no luck in the romance department, he decided to return to Menfro. *At least there I know folks and won't be so dang lonely,* he thought. *Might not be any good lookers there, but I can get some shuteye.*

The first night back in his old room in his parent's house, Cal figured he'd probably acted too quickly in deciding to move. While the new fangled lights and the commotion of the streetcars no longer disturbed him, he found that he still had difficulty going to sleep. Maybe it's the total darkness and quiet here. *What can I do? I couldn't get any rest when I was in the big burg. Now I can't get any back in this hick town*, he grumbled into his pillow.

Finally, he came up with what he believed the solution to his dilemma. He wouldn't live in either a small or large community but rather in a midsize one. To his great relief, his plan proved fruitful. Within a month of moving to Springfield, he was cured of his insomnia and had found the perfect mate. *Sometimes you just got to meet the problem halfway*, exulted Cal.

Precocious

Margo asked this question at 12: “If there is no God, why be a person of conscience?” It was shortly after that her parents began taking her to church.

On University Tenure

The university hires people it deems the best and six years later it fires them because they are.

#

The members of the tenure committee evaluated Carrie's bid for tenure and decided to grant it because they were confident she would not exceed their mediocrity.

#

The decision was split as to whether to grant a member of the department tenure. Half of the voting professors were against the candidate because they didn't like her, and the other half of the voting professors really didn't like her.

#

The awarding of tenure at the university was based on the following: 1.) Scholarly achievement, 2.) Excellence in teaching, and 3.) Service to the institution and department. On paper Professor Carlson met and, in fact, exceeded all criteria. However, the senior members in her discipline decided against her feeling she was too qualified for their own good.

The Passions of the Politically Correct

Swanson avidly consumed the remains of his chicken cutlet while noting to his fellow diners the inhumane treatment of poultry at the hands of breeders.

Police Protection

Hadley had a friend who was murdered by a serial killer. It was a particularly gruesome crime as homicides of this nature generally are. The perpetrator remained at large despite a major effort by law enforcement to apprehend him. Since the news of her friend's death, Hadley had lived in constant fear for her own life. Several photographs, including one of her, had been discovered missing from the scene of the atrocity. When Hadley learned of this from investigators, she was immediately convinced that she would be the killer's next victim. "What should I do?" she pleaded, and was told to stay vigilant and to keep her doors locked. This advice was a source of great comfort to her.

Wrong End of the Dial

Xylon Scib tuned into Earth's old-time radio shows via that planet's satellite service. Following ions of devoted listening, he decided that it was the place and era in which he'd most like to reside. He climbed into his time transporter for the jump across the universe. Seconds later he appeared at the NBC radio studios and was immediately confronted and shot by Jack Armstrong, The All-American Boy.

And Then a Rupture in the Universe

Geriatric researchers estimated it was around 2047 that the world's elderly population started to experience sudden age reversal. Indeed, people around sixty-five began appearing younger. However, despite intense investigations by Harvard, Oxford, and Johns Hopkins medical schools as to why seniors no longer assumed the typical signs of decline but instead grew youthful over a relatively short span of time, no definitive cause was found. Some scientists speculated that the answer to this vexing question might exist in the reactivation of telomerase, the enzyme that lengthens telomeres—prompting gene reproduction. While this dramatic change in the human condition pleased most elders, it upset their descendants who found themselves competing with their grandparents at job interviews and extreme sporting events.

What She Saw

When my sister's ex-husband suddenly died, she kept saying that every time she looked up at the sun, she saw his face. She told everybody that, and everybody thought she was just being Claudia. But recently she had become more peculiar than she'd always been—not wrapped too tight was the popular way of describing her. Within weeks after the funeral she was diagnosed with frontal lobe dementia, and her mental deterioration was fairly swift. Soon she stopped saying she could see her ex in the sun, because soon she stopped knowing what the sun was.

Bad Translation: French to English

Armand salua sa mere avec un baiser sur la joue et s'assit pour le petit dejeurner. Sur la table devant lui se trouvaient un verre de jus d'orange tout juste presse, un bol de muesli et un gateau aux framboises. Le garcon mangea lentement puis, s'excusant, revint a son instrument pour une autre heure de pratique.

Arnie ignored his mom as he stood at the kitchen counter and drank his orange soda, gulped down his Frosted Wheats, and chomped on his raspberry Pop Tart. He then went back to his room and continued playing his video game.

Splitting Hares

Josh had found an image on-line of a couple dressed in bunny costumes to send to his wife on Easter. She had a particular aversion to people in rabbit suits—"creepy," she had said—so he intended it as a joke. After he had emailed the jpeg, he dragged it to his trash, but it would not go in. "C'mon, get back into your rabbit hole, he muttered." He tried several more times and finally restarted his computer to see if it would clear up the glitch. It did not. *To hell with it*, he thought, and went on to something else. Later his wife came into his office and asked when he got her the new computer. He said he didn't know what she was talking about and went with her to her work area. Sure enough a new computer sat next to her old one. Josh explained that he had no idea how the second computer got there, and his wife waved him off with a sly smile and thanked him for the Easter gift. "It's very sweet of you, honey, knowing that my old computer needed to be replaced." Perplexed, Josh returned to his office only to find two new computers next to his year-old iMac. *What the . . . ? Okay, who's playing a joke on us?*" he wondered, and then looked at his computer's monitor. The bunny image that he could not get rid of was different than the one he had originally uploaded.

The new one displayed bunnies copulating. Suddenly he heard his wife shout his name, and he rushed to her. When he arrived on the scene, he found her standing before a row of new computers. “Look!” she cried out. *What’s going on? Every time I turn around there are more computers.* It was then that Josh figured out what was happening.

Lunch with Her

She orders a double extra dry Tangueray gin martini with three olives and rocks on the side. Some things never change, I think. I'm tempted to join her as I did in the old days but decide on a club soda with a wedge of lime. I need to hold onto my balance in this potentially volatile situation. I remind myself that we're here because of unfinished business stemming from property we co-own in Vermont. Yet the air is thick with tension and neither one of us knows quite what to say to the other. It's been a half dozen years since we parted company because of her countless infidelities. My rage has not dulled over time and still lurks just beneath the surface. It'll be difficult to keep it from asserting itself now that she's across from me and within easy striking distance. We both cover our faces with the menus until the handsome young waiter arrives. When he asks if we're ready to order, she looks up at him alluringly and says, "Yes, I'm *ravenous*."

When Told by a Friend He Would Never Want to Die in a Hospital . . .

Barry responded, "There are worse ways to go than hooked up to a ventilator. You could find yourself in the middle of an ocean with the fin of a shark moving toward you. How about bleeding out on a stretch of remote highway? Then there's falling out of a window onto a spiked fence. Would you prefer being blown to shreds by a terrorist? Or there's always getting tortured to death by a psychopath. You could . . . "

"Okay, okay!" interrupted his friend, "I'll take all of the IVs and wires, the humiliating physical probing, and the constant interruptions by doctors and nurses . . . Actually, come to think of it, tell me more about being in the middle of the ocean with the fin of a shark moving toward you."

Road Sage

Milos was deeply troubled by all the violence that was occurring on the highways. Each year the number of deadly confrontations between drivers had grown, and they were expected to continue at an alarming pace. As a person who prided himself on being a good citizen and community activist, he felt compelled to do something to reverse the horrible trend. It took him a while to come up with a plan, and when he did, he quickly set it in motion.

In less than a day Milos had come up with several anti-road rage slogans and plastered them all over his 2003 Toyota Corolla. Among the statements that adorned his car were:

Hey, stupid, cool it!

It's jerks like you that kill!

Slow down, clown!

Drive, don't fly, idiot!

Back away, fool!

Stop racing, dummy!

The next morning he began his road safety crusade. It involved driving his placard-laden automobile up and down the local interstate notorious for road rage incidents. Not long after he entered the highway he noticed that he was getting hostile looks from passing cars. *Well, I guess they're getting the message . . . good. Maybe they'll remember to behave rationally the next time something provokes them out here*, he thought. But before he reached the first exit, he was forced onto the shoulder by a vehicle that had been riding his bumper.

The usually unflappable Milos was surprised by the sudden hostility he felt as the driver that nearly collided with him ran up to his parked car. *Be calm, Milos*, he told himself. *Keep your senses about you. Don't . . .*

The State Highway Patrol dispatcher received a message that a man was being beaten about the head with a tire iron on the thruway, and she immediately sent a trooper to investigate. When the officer arrived on the scene, he found a bloodied and unconscious man on the ground next to his pickup truck.

A Bitter Sweet Experience

The donut isn't as sweet as he thought it would be, and he's somewhat disappointed. In fact, a second bite confirms that it's actually quite bland. He deserves a sweeter donut, he thinks, and returns to the donut shop. There he chooses a donut he's certain will be sweeter than the one he had. When he takes a bite of the new donut, he's very upset, because it's no sweeter than the first one. *Is this bakery trying to pull something over on me?* he wonders.

Memento Mori

I look at the grainy snapshot of Joyce, Gorgio, Lucia and Nora taken in a Paris club in the 1920s and think, *All many times gone . . . but still here.* Yes, John Updike, “No *momento mori* is so clinching as a photograph of a vanished crowd.”

Doubt

The Bachelorette is playing on the screen in front of me. I haven't bothered changing it and am irritated that a flight heading to Dubai would allow such puerile entertainment on its high end carriers. *You'd think they'd filter out this crap considering how offensive it must be to many people in this part of the world*, I think. The passenger next to me suddenly shifts in his seat and reaches under his *thawb* revealing a gun strapped to his leg. He catches my wide-eyed stare and gives me a hard look. I grow rigid in my seat and wonder what to do. Should I shout "terrorist!!" and hope other passengers will help me disarm him? He sees that I'm weighing the situation and presses his body against mine, his face inches away. My heart shudders and I'm certain the end is near, but the bearded stranger whispers that he's an air marshal. I nod in acknowledgment and feel myself relax, but then I wonder, *is he lying?*

Joy Williams

After finishing *ninety-nine stories of GOD*, I phone the author and ask why she gave the book that title since most of the pieces in it don't even mention God. When I sense she's about to say something, the line goes dead.

Is There a Sense of Humor in the Afterlife?

"You've *spent* your heaven, Mr. Clausen," declared St. Gabriel to the new arrival.

"What do you mean, sir? I've lived a righteous life, always careful to do the right and honorable thing. Don't I deserve entry?"

"Sorry . . . *no*, you don't. You've lived the 86 years of your life in the most advanced society on Earth, with all the comforts any human could want. You've never missed a meal, went without a roof over your head, suffered because of a lack of medical care . . ."

"I don't understand. I thought if a person lived according to the Good Book, he would gain admittance up here."

"Well, that's not how it works. Half of the planet's population has lived abject existences in the undeveloped countries, and they're the ones we allow in. Surely you can see the wisdom in that, Mr. Clausen."

"So, I'm going to burn in hell because I spent my life as a member of America's upper middle class?"

"Oh, no. You're going to trade places with those poor, wretched souls who gain admission into the Promised Land."

"Well, I guess that's only fair," admitted Mr. Clausen, resigned to his fate.

"Okay . . . *okay*," laughed Gabriel. "I was only bullshitting."

Sibling Accommodation

You know those little malted milk balls probably more popular in the 1950s than today? Well, they made me puke. Not the chocolate on the outside but the malt inside. There was something about the crusty centers that offended my taste buds and gave my gut spasms. My sisters loved them and knew I wouldn't try stealing any as I usually did with most of their sweets. Knowing I was no threat to these particular treats, they would taunt me by making loud, lip-smacking sounds as they devoured one malted milk ball after another. Finally, I came up with a plan to get even. When they weren't looking, I would suck the chocolate from the candies, leaving the dreaded centers intact. After an angry confrontation with my sisters when they saw what I had done, we arrived at a compromise. I could eat the chocolate outers and they would be content with the vile innards, which they actually preferred. When we grew into adulthood, our ability to meet halfway on issues fell by the wayside. I could not abide my sister's holier-than-thou attitude when it came to my skinning animals and leaving them the organs.

Critical

I'm reading Book Five of Karl Ove Knausgaard's critically acclaimed, *My Struggle*. It's over 600 pages. I'm on page 74, and I remind myself that this author has received much acclaim for his series of memoirs. I'm wondering if I should write a memoir based upon my experience reading these lumbering tomes. I could also call it *My Struggle*.

Divine Reasoning

Pa got a job selling the King James Version of the Bible door-to-door. It was the only thing he could find after he got out of jail for shoplifting. It was his second offense, so the judge gave him 60 days to think about what he'd done. Pa did think about it enough not to want to steal anything else from a store, but he found it hard to get a job because people around town knew what he'd done and didn't want to hire him. When the Bible Man, as Pa called him, came to town, it didn't matter to him what people had done in their past. All he cared about was selling as many of his expensive bibles in the month he planned to be in town. The first week Pa didn't sell any bibles, so we didn't have any money because he was only paid if he sold one. Two days into the second week, Pa said he'd had enough of trying to peddle the Holy Book and came up with an idea. He was going to borrow six of the bibles, and we were going to leave town and go some place where he could sell them for half price and keep all the money. Then he said we'd leave the area for good, and start our lives somewhere else brand new. He said God helped those who helped themselves.

There Are Perfectly Justifiable Reasons for Road Rage

The GPS indicated 8.4 miles to his destination with an estimated time of arrival of almost an hour. "God-damn traffic! What's going on? Must be a frigging accident or roadwork. Just like rush hour out here, and its *Sunday*, for bloody sakes . . . *Move*, schmuck! Shitty Boston drivers!" grumbled Josh, banging on his steering wheel. *I won't make it in time, he thought. Can't believe this is happening. Why, God . . . why? Am I asking too much? My luck has to be the worst in the world. Crap just seems to happen to me. By the time I get there, the KFC will be closed.*

The Suicide Calendar

Why take life seriously? You'll never get out of it alive.
Elbert Hubbard

Back when Avery Mandel was feeling desperately low, he designated a date when he would take his life if things didn't improve. Unfortunately they hadn't by the time the date arrived, but he couldn't bring himself to end his life. His finger froze on the gun's trigger as he held the barrel in his mouth, and after several minutes he gave up on the idea . . . at least for the moment.

Later that same afternoon, Avery decided on another date to terminate his existence—this one a month hence. However, when that date arrived, he still couldn't do it. *Goddamn it, you pathetic coward. You don't want to live, but you haven't got the gumption to take action to change things*, he groused, feeling more depressed than ever.

This went on for months until Avery reached the breaking point.

Okay, I'll definitely do it on the 31st of December, my birthday. End *of the year, too . . . symbolic*, he decided and marked that date on the calendar.

On the first day of his 36th year, he rose and went to his desk where he stored his 38-caliber handgun.

This is it. I'm really going to do it this time. Life is just a misery, and I can't take it anymore, he mumbled, placing the gun to his temple. *It's now or never, Avery. Things are never going to get better for you . . . not if you live to be a hundred.*

Avery pressed the trigger, but nothing happened. He dropped to his knees gasping for air and trembling. *Oh, my God! I'm not dead,* he thought, and then realized he had not loaded the gun.

"Son of a bitch, I'm screwed now!" he cried, dropping his pistol. "I don't have a *new* calendar."

Some Things Are Just Better off Than Other Things

According to the American Medical Association, nails, teeth, and hair are the only parts of the human body that can't get cancer.

Woman Is Always Mother to the Child

Fifty-nine year old Clarence Needham was waiting for his wife to pick him up at his doctor's office and trying hard to think of ways to keep from breaking out in tears when she showed up. *Bite the inner walls of your mouth*, he told himself, having done that to good effect countless times in the past. *Just don't look like a blubbering baby in the waiting room when she appears. She hates that side of you and will probably turn and walk right out if she sees that.* He thought about his wife's lack of compassion and began to grow angry. *I've just been told I'm going to have to have surgery, and she'll get pissed at me and call me a wimp because I'm all upset. Well, screw her.* By the time his wife did appear, Clarence had become so agitated by what he felt was his wife's insensitivity and his impending medical procedure that he lost his resolve to control his emotions and burst out crying. "For heavens sake, Clarence, stop that! You're acting like a little boy," growled Mrs. Needham. "Yeah, a little boy who has to have *surgery*," he managed to reply between sobs. "What? Oh, my God, what kind?" After a lengthy pause, during which he labored to catch his breath, he answered, "I have to have my tonsils out."

Synchronicity

It just occurred to me that I might go when my new dog does. I'm 70 and she's a pup with a life expectancy of 12-15 years. That puts us old and decrepit at the same time. What a nice bit of timing . . . the two of us leaving together.

“In Absentia”

Hey, Jake, you remember that old photo of the crowd downtown on Mulberry Street in Little Italy? What was it? VJ Day, I think . . . right? There’s a bunch of people on the building’s fire escape, and mom is standing below them. She’s the kid in the checkered dress waving a little flag as a ton of confetti is dropping from the sky. Next to her is her dad, our grandpa. You were only three when he passed, so you didn’t get to know him. He has his old army uniform from WW1 on even though all the other guys are in their shirtsleeves. Grandma isn’t in the shot because she died two months before from a broken neck when she fell down some stairs where they lived. Mom says that even though she’s got this big grin on her face watching the parade coming, all her happiness left when grandma did. Wish I could find that damn picture.

The Never Ending Story

It's 1931 and the marquee of the RKO Mayfair on Seventh Avenue brightens the night with the words:

NOW OPEN
THE NEW
DELUXE R-K-O
THEATRE
CONSTANCE
BENNETT
SIN TAKES
A HOLIDAY
POPULAR PRICES
CONTINUOUS

Benny Novak stares up at the two-story sign and scratches his head. He's confused by something it says and walks over to the ticket window.

"What's 'continuous'?" he asks the young woman in the booth.

"Huh?" she replies.

"The sign says 'continuous.' What's 'continuous'?"

"Continuous'?" responds the baffled ticket-seller.

"Up there. It says 'continuous,'" persists Benny, pointing skyward.

"I can't see what you're talking about from in here."

"Well, how 'bout you come out and look?"

"I can't leave my station, sir. It's a rule. I'll get in trouble."

"Hey, I ain't gonna buy no ticket if you ain't gonna tell me what 'continuous' means."

"Oh, I know," declares the woman, suddenly catching on. "It means the movie just keeps going . . . *continues.* It never stops. You want a ticket?"

"You kiddin'? Never stops? Hell. I ain't got that much time, girlie."

Maternal Caution

If you let your hand dangle over the side of the bed, something under it may grab it, warned my mother when she was alive and I was little. So I pull it away when I remember her words, but it's too late because her icy fingers already have it.

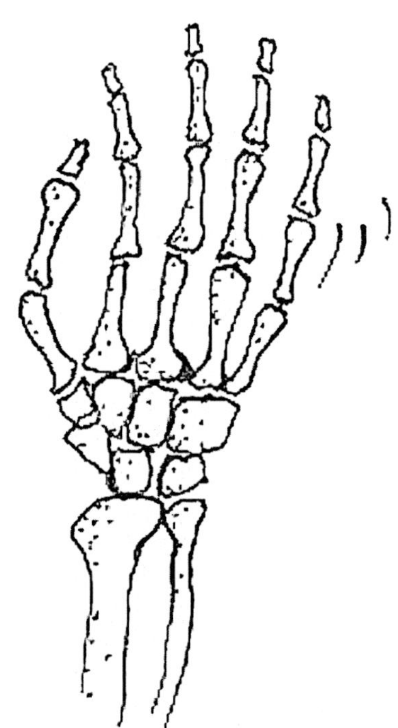

Virtually . . . *Not* Literally

"No," said the professor, "The Cloud is not actually located in the sky. It's not like it exists in the mist. I mean things are not uploaded into space. They're connected through the Internet. It's all wired and never really airborne, except when it's accessed via Wi-Fi."

The student looked at him skeptically, "So when someone says they sent something to the Cloud, they aren't actually sending something *up* at all?"

"Correct," replied the professor, thinking the dull-eyed, bleach-blond sophomore was finally grasping what he'd been attempting to convey to her for the better part of his office hour.

"Oh, so it's not out there," muttered the girl, glancing upward.

"Indeed, the term has to do with preserving information and data in a physical infrastructure that doesn't really exist in the air."

"Well, I think I get it, but wouldn't it be a lot less confusing and a whole lot more accurate if they just called it *ground* storage."

"I suppose that makes sense. Another term in use for the Cloud is data farms."

"Farms? Like where they grow things?" asked the bewildered student.

"Okay, I see it's time for my next lecture. You can leave now . . . *please*," said the professor, pointing toward the door.

The Inspiration and Curse of the Superior Talent

Is everybody else under the spell of Lydia Davis? Do you stop reading and dash to your keyboard because she's once again activated something in you? Have you written a piece that's still inferior to everything she's ever written?

There Was This Crazy Street Lady the Other Day

What she sees is a large fox chasing a cottontail rabbit up the side of a mustard jar that is so tall that its top is shrouded in green clouds. She figures if she yells at the fox she might save the poor little rabbit. So she shrieks, "Don't hurt that fucking bunny!" and it succeeds in distracting the hungry predator, which then turns and fixes its wild eyes on her and charges. The crazy street lady collapses to the pavement in horror but no one cares to save her. There is only revulsion on the faces of the passersby.

Animal Behavior

My husband and I wage war over whether we should get a cat or a dog. My preference is a cat because they don't require the care and attention that a dog does. He loves dogs because he grew up with one, and he says they bond with humans much better than cats. Furthermore, he says they're a good defense against break-ins. I counter this by reminding him that we live in a neighborhood that is virtually crime free. "Besides cats pretty much care for themselves," I say, "You don't have to walk them twice a day and worry about them biting someone." This debate goes on for weeks until I can no longer take the tension it has caused in our marriage. "Okay," I relent, "Let's get a dog." He looks surprised but not as happy as I expected. "What's the problem?" I ask, and he replies that he's thought it over and feels that I was right about a dog being a big responsibility, especially since we like to travel. "No, really, go ahead, get a dog. It's what you want," I insist, adding, "We can find a kennel to board him when we go away." He shakes his head no and suggests we go to the local animal rescue facility and choose a cat we both like. While I'm impressed that he's come around to my way of thinking, I sense that he'll never be happy if we don't get a dog. "No, we really should get a dog,"

I say, and he says, "Really, you sure? Hey, we can get a cat next," he offers, and I ask what he means by 'next. "You know, when the dog dies." Now the question is whether we should get a big dog or small one. He favors a large dog and I want one I can cuddle in my lap. We go back and forth on this and reach another impasse. Again, I give in and say I'm okay with what he wants, that I'll get used to a giant mutt if it makes him happy. "No, no," he says, "You got to be a hundred percent with this, because it's a major commitment." I tell him that my mind has changed on the subject and that I'd really like the biggest dog we can get. "No way," he says, and I say, "Way." After checking out a bunch of area shelters, we come up empty and decide we need to go to a breeder. I suggest we get a Bernese Mountain Dog, having researched the lifespans of K9s. He's thrilled with my suggestion. Five-and-a-half years later, we adopt a Siamese kitten.

Famous Intellectuals Debate and a Threat of Physical Violence Ensues*

Vidal: "Shut up a minute . . ."

Buckley: No, I won't . . . "

Vidal: "You're a pro-war, crypto-Nazi . . ."

Buckley: "Stop calling me a crypto-Nazi or I'll knock you in the goddamn face . . ."

* Excerpt from the televised 1968 Democratic convention debate featuring William F. Buckley and Gore Vidal.

When You're Not with the One You Love . . .

Constantine finished packing and prepared to check-out out of the motel and drive to Taos. *It'll take about seven hours to get there. Can't wait to see Maggie. It's been so long. God, do I need to get frisky with that gal,* he thought. When he reached Trinidad, he stopped for lunch. *I'm on schedule. Let me give Magpie a buzz and let her know.* The phone rang several times before a breathless voiced answered.

"That you, babe?" he asked.

"Yeah, it's me," replied Maggie, tentatively.

Constantine thought he heard a man's voice in the background.

"Someone there, Mag?"

"Huh? No . . . of course not."

Despite her denial, Constantine was certain his girlfriend was not alone. "What's going on? I know what I heard."

"It's the TV. Some detective show," said Maggie.

He was not buying it but decided not to pursue it any further until he saw her. When he arrived at her house, he immediately confronted her about the male voice he'd heard on the phone.

"Okay . . . okay. There is someone else. You're gone so much, I decided to buy an X410 Male Companion Bot."

"Whew! Damn, Maggie, I thought there was another person with you," replied Constantine, with a sigh of relief.

Don't Try This at Home

Nine-year old Peter had seen clowns at the circus perform some amazing stunts, but the one that impressed him the most involved one clown bending over and putting his hands between his legs while another clown pulled on them and flipped him upright. *I bet I can do that*, he thought, while playing in his backyard with his best friend, Brian. "All you do is yank on my hands real hard," he told his playmate, as he bent over in front of him. "I don't know," hesitated Brian, who eventually was cajoled into giving the trick a go. "Now pull real hard," said Peter, clasping his friend's hands and bracing to be twirled upside down. "Ready," asked Brian? "Yup," replied Peter, taking a deep breath. For a split second, he saw everything around him spiral. When he regained consciousness a week later, he despaired at not having landed on his feet like Freckles had.

Plein Air

Marcel took the Tea Train to Alve where he set up his easel on the Rue Daphne to paint the rats behind Café Lucien.

When Less Became More

A less famous writer invited a more famous writer to his house for the weekend. The more famous writer wrote murder mysteries and had generously praised his host in a book review that provided the lesser-known writer much-needed attention. Thus a friendship had ensued. After the weekend, the more famous writer decided to stay on for a few more days, which turned into a few more weeks. The less famous writer became eager to see the more famous writer leave. It wasn't that he was bad company. It was just that he interfered with the less famous writer's solitude, which he needed to write his less successful works. When six months had passed, the less famous writer decided the only way to get rid of the more famous writer was to kill him like the more famous writer had a character in one of his bestselling novels. The less famous writer committed the murder as penned by the more famous writer and was caught and prosecuted for his dark deed. He thus became more famous than his former more famous writer houseguest.

Small Dangers

We're in a remote village in the southern region of Tanzania. Our guide is showing us the inside of a lean-to when he spots a scorpion. He shouts for us to stand still. We don't see the dreaded creature but we're horrified nonetheless. "Where is it?" I ask tremulously, and he points to the dirt floor a couple feet from where we're all standing. I see something that looks like a tiny cricket with an erection and wonder how something that appears so insignificant can be so harmful. Our guide says that the smaller the scorpion the bigger the hurt you get from it. Size *does* matter. "The little fuckers can kill you," he adds, and stamps on it. When he lifts his sandaled foot there is no evidence of the predator that had sat in waiting for us.

Wound Dresser

Whitman brings them candy, books, and solace as their injuries from the uncivil war fester and resist healing. He loves their youth and listens to their battlefield accounts as intently as any minister or parent would. The great army of the sick relentlessly fills hospitals with its maimed and distressed as the bard of democracy holds vigils for the countless dying. Later at his makeshift desk in the embalming station he sets to paper the tears that have accumulated in his quill.

Published Author

You write your heart out for a year and send your work to a tiny indie publisher that welcomes unsolicited manuscripts. Weeks pass and you cling to the hope that your fiction will have a life between covers. In the meantime, you read countless other authors and come to believe they are light years better than you. You begin to feel your optimism fade. But, finally, you hear back from the press you submitted to and are told that if you purchase 200 copies of your novel (which you've titled "Midnight Harbor") and assume responsibility for its marketing and promotion, they would be more than delighted to offer you a contract for "Midnight Harkens."

A Lifelong Mystery

When I was little I slept with my father because we never had more than one bedroom. Actually, we seldom had more than one room wherever we lived . . . and we lived in a lot of places. That was because he was an alcoholic and never kept a job. He started drinking when my mother was killed in a car accident, and that happened when I was just three years old. I never minded sleeping in the same bed with him, because that's pretty much how it always was and it seemed normal. The only thing I felt funny about was that he didn't wear underpants to bed, and sometimes my hand would accidentally brush against his naked buttocks. He never said anything because he was probably asleep. I sure didn't say anything and tried hard to steer clear of his rump in what was sometimes just a single bed. I've never really understood why someone would keep his undershirt on but not wear his shorts to bed.

Life Goes On

"Saw this photo the other day taken in the Ukraine back in the 30s. All these kids were starving to death. They looked like skeletons. Really disgusted me," said James.

"Yeah, I saw a picture in an old magazine of this Russian soldier frozen in place in Finland during the War. Even though I don't like the Ruskies, I couldn't help but think the guy had people who loved him somewhere," added Carmine.

"A photo in *Newsweek* of these people jumping to their deaths from the top floor of a burning building made me sick to my stomach. Should have seen the terror in their faces," observed Leo.

"Came upon this snapshot of an amusement park ride that had collapsed and took all these riders with it. There were bloody bodies all over the place," offered Chuck.

"You catch that photo in the *Herald* last week of the car wreck on Ames Street with that body hanging through the windshield?" asked Benny.

"I've always been bugged by a picture of Nazis executing all those folks in the trenches they made them dig," commented Frank.

"You ever see that shot of the Chinese kid carrying his dead brother on his back to a cremation site? That one always makes me feel awful," admitted Ryan.

"That pic of the Indian tsunami victims floating on the river was as creepy as they get and sticks in my mind," conveyed Jess.

"C'mon, enough with the small talk, you guys. Who wants another beer?" blurted Kevin.

Getting It Write

Will feared his prose was pretentious. It worried him that it might lack grit and candor. He took this mindset to his next story, reminding himself what Hemingway had recommended—"Write one true sentence." *Okay, let's do that.* Thus he began:

"The world can be a very cruel place . . ."

At his next writing group, he was praised for his veracity but criticized for his cynicism.

When Lost Valor Finds Another Host

We huddle in the corner of the storm cellar. It's pitch black and all I can hear is our nervous breathing. Daddy covers us with his body and tells us everything will be okay. Then there's a terrible roar and the ground shakes. My little sister begins to cry, and I'm on the verge of doing the same. I hold back because I'm older and need to show courage. Suddenly the shelter door begins to rattle and Daddy runs to it and tries to hold it shut. His strength is no match against the ferocious wind that rips the wooden entrance from its hinges and lifts Daddy into the darkness. We scream for him and then suddenly everything grows still like somebody's hit a switch. I begin to sob and my baby sister puts her arms around me and says everything will be okay, adding, "Let's go find Daddy."

Moveable Beast

The wasted dog drags away the carcass it has lucked upon at the edge of the dry riverbed. Flies cling to it and a vulture circles low. When the mutt has reached its patch of shade, it rips into the dead thing and gulps down a mouthful of maggots contentedly.

My Parents Always Said Not to Make Fun of the Elderly

Dark Things Rise from the Senior Body

The dull morning light seeps through the motel window. My wife does her stretches as I stagger to the bathroom to relieve myself. I catch my image in the mirror and discover that somehow in the course of the night a foot long ear hair has sprung from my head. I wrap it around my drooping lobe to show my wife. After I've emptied my bladder, I start to walk from the bathroom but am pulled backward and end up on my ass. My ear feels like someone has stabbed it. When I stand, I see the wispy follicle move across the floor, climb to the sink, and slip down the drain. This is not the first time this has happened, and I think that getting old is an alien thing.

* * *

Born Too Soon

If old age was 140, we'd be fine at 80.
But it isn't . . . and we're not.
What if it were though? Just saying . . .
You wouldn't think so little of us at 80,
Would you . . . if old age was 140?

Getting Sick at the South Pole

"I have nightmares about catching an infection in Antarctica, so I'm just not going there," declared the soon-to-be centenarian when asked what she planned to do on her birthday.

* * *

Adjusting Life Expectancy

An article on WebMed recommended that old people put on 15 to 20 pounds above their normal weight because it could help stave off the grim reaper in the last period of life. The Carson's took this advice to heart. But Mr. Carson gained 50 extra pounds thinking he'd outlive his wife and thereby get to enjoy more time in what was their only bathroom. It was there he was forced to spend most of his remaining days after she passed.

* * *

Senior Sleep

Fitful, intermittent, sporadic, broken, disturbed, patchy, irregular, uneven, desultory, periodic, spotty, flickering, haphazard, hit-or-miss, interrupted, erratic, fragmentary . . . *fuck it!*

Caution

When you encounter old people, be aware that they often feel the way they look.

* * *

Age Is an Insensitive Bastard, Because . . .

We all end up one thousand pound manatees.

* * *

Old

My skin is like parchment. Draw on me, and you will draw blood.

* * *

A Question That Is Almost Always Answered in the Affirmative

"Are you afraid of dying?"

Shoes

Mrs. Mayberry insisted that her five male boarders remove their shoes and leave them in the vestibule before entering the house. This made it easy to determine who was home at any given time—what pair belonged to our fellow tenants was something we learned quickly, too. We were all pretty friendly with each other and about the same age—in our 20s. Our landlady had lost her son around that age, so she liked to rent to young men. She said it gave her comfort to have us around. One snowy evening I came in from work and found everybody already home. However, along with my pair of shoes I counted five others. When I went into the common room, all four of the other roomers were there reading and listening to the radio . . . Arch Oboler's "Lights Out" was on. I looked around for the person belonging to the additional shoes but saw no one else. Mrs. Mayberry must have a guest, I figured, but then she entered the room unaccompanied. "Whose extra pair of shoes in the foyer?" I asked. "What do you mean?" said Mrs. Mayberry. "There should only be five pair. I don't leave my shoes out there . . . so just five." I repeated my claim that there was an extra pair of shoes where there should only be five, and she headed to the front door with all of us trailing her. When she reached the line of shoes, she gave out a loud gasp. “Whose idea of a cruel joke is it to put my dead son’s wing tips out here?”

Judy, Judy, Judy

When I was nine, my father took me to see "North by Northwest," starring Cary Grant. I really liked Cary Grant and began doing impressions of him by squinting and talking between my teeth. I didn't tell people I was impersonating Cary, because I wanted them to figure that out on their own. Most of all I hoped they would think I looked like the handsome 55 year-old actor.

The New Normal

Marty circled a date on the calendar when he'd begin his diet. He really wanted to drop some bulk before his annual physical five months hence but knew that was probably not going to happen. *Okay, maybe 20 pounds*, he thought, and then lowered his goal to 10. Finally, he figured if he could just remain at the weight of his last physical exam, he would have achieved something. When the date of his physical arrived, he reluctantly climbed onto the scale. "Two hundred eighty-seven pounds," announced the nurse. Marty's heart sank, because he was one pound over last year's weigh in. When the doctor entered the exam room, he congratulated Marty. "You've hardly gained anything since last time. Good for you. At this new rate, by the time you hit 60, you'll only be 50 pounds overweight. Considering the American diet, that's about right."

Christopher Hitchens Meets God

Hitchens: “Well, I can see that I was wrong.”

God: “No, the evidence was weak. My bad!”

An Awful Lot of Nudity

The rating box in the ad for the movie stated "Mild violence, some language, and an awful lot of nudity."

"You see this?" asked Mel.

"What?" replied his friend.

"This flick says it has 'an awful lot of nudity.'"

"Huh? C'mon, man. Let me see. They never say that."

"Well, that's what it says. Look, 'an awful lot of nudity.'"

"Oh my God, you're right. That's so cool."

"What's the picture about? Never heard of it."

"Who cares? It's got to be great with 'an awful lot of nudity,' *right*?"

"Shit yes!" answered Mel.

Mama Said It Was His Special Place, but She Didn't Know Why

At least twice a year, Daddy would take my baby sister and me on a Sunday ride to Tryon. It was an hour drive from our house in North Platte, and along the way we'd stop for a picnic lunch in a field with a big Cottonwood tree. As soon as we got to Tryon, Daddy would turn the car around and we'd head home. We didn't mind going there so many times, but when we got a little older we asked why he always took us to the same place. "'Cause there's just no place nicer than Tryon," he answered.

Late Reading

Under the canvas top of a deuce-and-a-half US army truck serving as the 31st Division's Mobile Library, GI's fresh off of the battlefield check out Remarque's *All Quiet on the Western Front*, Twain's *War Prayer*, Hemingway's *A Farewell to Arms*, Trumbo's *Johnny Got His Gun*, Stephen Crane's *The Red Badge of Courage*, Dos Passos's *Three Soldiers*, and other anti-war novels as a diversion from the carnage they have witnessed and wrought.

America Runs on Dunkin

When I'm in other parts of the country where there's hardly any Dunkin Donuts, or even none at all, my morning is messed up. My head and body are off track the rest of the day. I'm really sluggish and slower thinking than usual. As soon as I get back to Dunkin Country—New England—things fall back into focus. My morning stop at DDs is a ritual, as it is for nearly everyone I know. I've decided that I'm not going on trips where there isn't any Dunkins. They don't have to be on every corner like they are in Boston, but they have to be somewhere I can get to. I'll drive a few miles for my morning Dark Roast and Coffee Cake Muffin, no sweat. It bums me that France has no Dunkin Donuts, because my wife really wants to go there. Figure it's probably an anti-American thing. Maybe the government is afraid that once its citizens taste DDs delicious croissants it will have a revolution on its hands? The guys I meet each morning at Dunkin think that's the reason. It's a shame considering everything we did for the froggies in WWII.

Invisible Youth

Curious about what Irish novelist William Trevor looked like as a young man, I Google him and find he is only recalled in pictures as a senior citizen. *Was he born old?* I wonder.

Once Prolific

This author is really good, I think, and check out his bibliography in the front matter of the paperback. I notice its copyright date and I'm surprised the book is five years old, because I was under the impression it was new when I ordered it from Amazon. The title had caught my attention when I was checking out the catalog of a press to which I was considering submitting my own first manuscript of stories. A couple hours later, I've read all but two pieces in the collection and am more impressed by the writer than ever. The author's bio on the back cover is brief, so I Google him for more information. He's written a lot and I calculate by his date of his birth that he's 18 years younger than I am. A wave of envy sweeps over me, and then I notice that the Wikipedia entry on him is using the past tense—he *was*. Something keeps me from finishing the book.

When They Realize They Have No Real Grievance

She says, "I do most of the cleaning."

He says, "*Indoors* you do."

"That's right, indoors," she says, "And you do very little."

"I do most of the cleaning *outdoors*," he says, "And you do very little."

They stare at each other for a moment and then go in their respective directions.

Ring Tones

The loud ringing in Harold's ears had become a major distraction. There was no quiet time in his life anymore. When it began a few years earlier, it was just white noise and something he was seldom aware of unless there were no other sounds around him. His doctor called it Tinnitus and suggested he go to an audiologist, which he did not. "At this age they have you going to a specialist for every damn thing you complain about," he bemoaned at his men's reading group. A few members claimed they, too, suffered from the affliction and one made an intriguing statement. "If you concentrate hard enough, you can change the noise to something pleasant. Listen to what you like and try to meld your thoughts with it . . . kind of like in *Star Trek*. It's what I did, and I managed to change the ringing to a Mozart piano concerto . . . *sotto voce*. Hey, it could work for you, too." When Harold returned home, he considered his friend's suggestion. *A lovely violin piece by Vivaldi . . . actually anything but this infernal swooshing and buzzing. Maybe if I leave the radio on while I'm sleeping something will displace this aggravating racket. God, if only it would . . .* Harold dialed the classical music station he was fond of and slowly drifted off to sleep. The next morning, a middle C and

C sharp above jerked him from an unsettling dream. It was if someone had squeezed lemons into his ears. *Ugh . . . Arnold Schoenberg! I hate his stuff.* Harold hit the off switch on his Bose, but the cacophony continued. Shit, what's the problem? He then pulled the cord from its outlet but the acerbic notes continued to fill the air. After several moments, he let out a sigh of resignation. *Well*, he thought, *I guess my Tinnitus is gone.*

Advertisement in *The Mortuary Times*

"In addition to our standard body bags, Cadaver Products Unlimited offers chlorine free, disaster & transport, and outbreak response bags. We also have toe tags and ID kits, casket covers, water recovery carriers, corpse shrouds, and disaster pouches. Limited time offer on disposable polyethylene aprons, boot covers, full-face splash shields, odor neutralizer, clear oculist eye caps, expression mouth formers, and Frigid body sprays. Bulk discounts available in time for the holidays."

Just When You Think Things Can't . . .

Egan always took a seat in the back of the classroom and at the most remote table in the cafeteria. He considered it fortunate whenever he was able to avoid being seen by the other students. What they thought of him was amply clear. In their eyes, he was grotesque . . . not even worthy of bullying anymore. A rumor had been spread that he had leprosy or some other type of contagious skin disease, and he could see the fear in kid's expressions when they inadvertently made eye contact with him. The ones he hated most were those with flawless complexions—those without pimples or blemishes. They were few in number in the age of junk food and super sized drinks, and he knew exactly who they were. He'd watched them with envy and resentment since entering high school. At night in his room, he plotted to spoil their perfect little faces. *Acid is the best way to do it*, he told himself, and set about acquiring the necessary solution to accomplish his deed. When the day came to launch his campaign of revenge, Egan concealed the bottle of disfiguring liquid in his briefs. On the way to school, the warmth and smoothness of the container stimulated his penis, causing the vessel to uncork and spill just as he reached the campus. Egan fell to the ground writhing in indescribable pain, his hands clutching at his crotch. His screams drew a small crowd of students, but no one came to his aid. They just looked on and snickered. "Look, Igor is jerking off." When his agony abated enough so that he could stand, he limped home and took a long, soothing shower. As he toweled off, he caught his image in the mirror. His phallus and testicles were gone. *Okay*, he thought, *things just got worse* ...

Where Art Thou, Morpheus?

It's past midnight and I toss and turn. *Shit . . . shit!* This just isn't going to work, I tell myself, knowing I'm no closer to catching my eight hours than I was the night before or the night before that. I could always get a prescription for one of those sleep aids you see advertised on TV, like Ambien, Lunesta, Rozerem, Sonata, or Restoril, but I don't want to get hooked. It can happen. Some of my friends are really dependent on them. So I toss and turn and fret that I'll never have another normal night's sleep . . . or a day with lucid thoughts. I wish for nothing more than some solid shut-eye. I even pray for it, although I'm not what you'd call religious. Then it finally comes out of the blue as I'm speeding down the highway at 80 miles per hour. And there I am, finally unconscious. Prayers answered.

Mister Insensitive

We're blind to our blindness.
We have very little idea of how little we know.
Daniel Kahneman

"If you're diagnosed with a rare cancer, is that supposed to make you feel special?" asked Gail, trying to put the best face possible on what her doctor just told her.

Unaware that this was not just an oddball question, her boyfriend, Burt, replied, "I suppose it depends on just *how* rare the cancer is."

"Let's say it's very rare and incurable," said Gail, still trying to appear nonchalant but on the verge of tears.

"Well, in that case, you'd have to feel *very* special," chuckled Burt, as he took a generous bite from his meatball sub.

"Asshole!" cried Gail, rising from the table and running from the sandwich shop.

Burt watched through the window as she disappeared down the street. *Christ, what was that all about? Women are so freaky at times. The littlest thing sets them off,* he thought, stuffing a handful of cheese fries into his mouth.

That evening Gail called her boyfriend and apologized for her behavior, saying that it had been a tough day. When Burt asked her about it, she began to cry.

"Wow, babe, chill. It couldn't have been that bad. You get so upset about nothing sometimes. So what's the problem *this* time?"

The next thing Burt heard was a dial tone. *Must be on her period*, he figured and went back to watching the game.

When the phone rang early the next morning, Burt ignored it thinking it was probably Gail. *Not going to deal with her today. Let her get over her wacky mood swings*. He let the phone ring a couple more times during the day, and then finally answered it when it rang that evening.

"You over the crazies, lady?" he said, before Gail could speak.

There was no response, and he hung up. It was the last time he ever heard from her. Burt thought about Gail occasionally and then she left his thoughts entirely.

Assisted Living

Long unable to rise on my own from my wheelchair, a sudden impulse has me doing back flips across the rec room floor. The other seniors stare in amazement and then applaud. I bow appreciatively and then demonstrate other acts that involve extraordinary balance, agility and motor coordination. My performance arouses the notice of two attendants, who shout at me to stop what I'm doing. "You'll hurt yourself, Mildred!" they say, and I wake up from my power nap.

Strangers on a Train

Sri Lankan geologist Indra de Silva strikes up a conversation with writer Amy Hempel as they travel from Rome to Paris. "Would I know anything you've written?" asks de Silva. "Maybe, if you like stories that probe the human condition in all of its varied and compelling manifestations," answers Sempel." "No, I'm not a big fan of fiction," shrugs de Silva, returning to his copy of Gem and Rock Magazine.

A Question of Minimal Urgency

Given the billions of observable planets that exist, do you think it's likely there's a species out there that does not have to excrete body waste?

Willy Is Pleased That eBay Exists

He bought an expensive piano on credit because he pledged to himself that he would finally learn to play a musical instrument.

Due Process

The garden appeared empty, so I snuck a rose to give to my girlfriend. As I was about to continue to her house, a cop stopped me and asked for my ID. "Why am I being stopped, officer?" I asked, and he said for vandalizing a public space and for resisting arrest. "What *vandalizing* and what *resisting* arrest?" I blurted in disbelief. "Turn around and put your hands behind your back," he ordered. I attempted to hand him the flower to hold and he shouted FREEZE, firing off his Taser. I was cuffed on the ground and then put into the cruiser. I was so shocked by what was happening that I didn't recognize the black face looking back at me in the rearview mirror.

An Example of Ernst's Grim Preoccupation

How many bodies are being taken to the morgue in the hospitals of Berlin today? he wondered, while eating a third spritzkuchen.

But Words Will Never Harm Me

I try to deny myself illusions or delusions, and I think that this perhaps entitles me to try and deny the same to others, as long as they refuse to keep their fantasies to themselves.
Christopher Hitchens

People were clearly not reading Barry Cliff's short stories online or purchasing his books the way they had when he began to publish. Of late, he received little response when he posted a new work on social media—the number of "likes" they got on Facebook had dwindled. This puzzled and frustrated Barry and prompted him to question the content and nature of his tales. Yes, they were clearly quite dark and typically condemning of the human condition, but that had been his intent.

"People don't like to read gloomy stories, even if they contain basic truths," offered his friend and fellow writer, Zak Berman, when Barry complained about his nearly non-existent readership.

"My fiction conveys the sad facts about life and its tragic realities. I feel an author should write what he feels and do so with conviction, even if his words are hard to swallow and disturb people."

"Well, I agree with that, but writers have to deal with the consequences of their views. You write stories that are pretty depressing. People would prefer not to face the bleaker aspects of existence. Your pieces contain themes that are upsetting to the average reader, so folks avoid them . . . even though what you do is well written and possesses real merit. In the end, attacking people's faith and debunking their beliefs is going to turn them off, Barry."

"I'm not *attacking* anyone's beliefs. I'm simply putting forth my position on the ridiculous dogma that plagues our society."

"Don't be defensive, Barry. I'm just giving you my views on the subject. You asked for my thoughts."

"I'm not being defensive, but what you're saying, Zak, is that I should lighten up if I want to attract more readers? In other words, be more warm and fuzzy, right?"

"No, I'm *not* saying you should fill your prose with uplifting platitudes and sentimental plots. You must be you and not compromise your vision for the sake of a bigger audience. But if it bugs you that you're not being read, maybe you should add a little more cheer and hopefulness in your stories. You don't have to be

Dave Barry or Nicholas Sparks, but a little chuckle and some positivity go a long way."

Barry contemplated Zak's suggestions and decided to steer his writing in a more life-affirming direction. *I think I can do that and get my essential message across to the reader*, he thought. *I won't be selling out, and maybe I will appeal to a larger audience.*

The first thing he wrote that embraced this new mindset was a piece optimistically entitled: A *World of Goodness*. The opening paragraph reflected the tone and spirit of the entire story:

> The sun rose and washed the porch in a golden glow. Although Calvin could not see the spectacular sunrise because he was blind, he appreciated the warmth that accompanied it as he sat in his wheelchair paralyzed from the waist down. *God is great*, thought Calvin, *even if I was born without the sight to witness His magnificent creations or the ability to walk among them . . .*

Barry's new story failed to win him a broader fan base, and the reaction to it by his friend, Zak, fell significantly short of his expectations.

A Father's Legacy

Ever since he saw *Psycho* when he was a kid, Monroe has locked the door to the bathroom. He knows it's silly, especially since his wife and kids are generally in the house, but he can't break the 40-year long habit. He keeps a wary eye out for shadows beyond the shower curtain and listens for any suspicious sounds. Because he is in a hurry one day, he fails to bolt the bathroom door. As he's lathering up, he notices a shadow moving swiftly in his direction. He gives out a blood-curdling scream and leaps through the vinyl curtain landing on the intruder. Now his son locks the bathroom door when he takes a shower.

How Derrick Lost Something, Found it, and Lost It Again

On my way from my den, I set my coffee cup on the bookshelf. My wife has summoned me, and I go to the front room where she is cleaning.

"Can you reach that cobweb up there in the corner with the duster?" she asks, and I do her bidding.

"Anything else?" I ask, and she points to another ceiling corner with a cobweb.

I take care of it, and she thanks me. Halfway back to my home office, I realize I don't have my coffee, and try to think where I put it. I scan the family room and then the dining room. Zilch. *Where the hell is it?* I grumble, and I look on the porch where I do most of my reading during the hot days of summer. I'd been out there in the morning taking advantage of the dawn's coolness while reading my Stephen King novel. *Nothing out here . . . shit! Can't believe how absentminded I am.*

After a few more moments trying to reconstruct my movements, I return to the front room where my wife is now Windexing the glass in the frames of our family photographs. "Did you see where I set my coffee?"

I ask her, and she shakes her head no. *Sonofabitch*!

Next, I retrace my steps, closely surveying each room I'd passed through on my way to the other end of the house. Then it occurs to me, *Crap, it was the last of the coffee in the pot, too. Shit! shit! shit!*

For the next quarter hour or so, I prowl about looking for my special monogrammed mug but come up empty. *Just like that, poof, it's gone? How is that possible?* I ask myself, fighting back the urge to defile something . . . kick the furniture, punch the wall. *Screw it! I don't need it. Had a few sips. I'll survive*, I mutter, reentering my office.

Inside the door, I spot my cup. *Right where you left it . . . a-hole.* I grab it and take a gulp of its contents. *Fuck, it's cold!* I yell, and heave the mug my daughter gave me for my birthday across the room.

Lost Poets

It is estimated that hundreds of thousands of people have published verse. How many can you name?

Bad DIY Idea

"Your face is falling away from your skull. That's why you look older. The tissue's underpinning is giving way resulting in geriatric sag. This gets worse every year until you end up looking like a Shar-Pei," said Dr. Goldfarb.

"Oh, that's terrible," moaned Mrs. Hebe, inspecting the large bags under her eyes in the magnified mirror.

"We can staple you back if you don't want surgery, but this only holds for a while. Again, I would suggest a full facelift. It will give you what you want, and it will last longer than the alternatives. It's your decision, Mrs. Hebe. So what do you want to do?" asked the plastic surgeon.

"Well, I'm not going under the knife, so I'll go with the other option you mentioned. Besides, it will be a lot cheaper."

"Not really *that* much cheaper . . . "

"Of course it will be, doctor!" protested Mrs. Hebe. "I have a stapler at home."

From Ashes to Ashes

When the extraterrestrials informed us that in addition to all of the wonderful things they brought to the human species they could resurrect the dead, most people were beside themselves with joy. The prospect of seeing deceased relatives, friends, and lovers was beyond imagining. However, when the aliens revealed that they could not bring back those who had been cremated, a third of the world's population was deeply disappointed. To add to their chagrin, Orthodox Jews, Muslims, and Presbyterians boasted that they had known that all along.

Heartfelt Concern

Whenever I lean back on the couch watching the tube, my heart begins to beat really weird. First it seems like it's moving sideways, and then it lurches up and down. If I bend forward slightly, it starts getting back to a regular rhythm, although not quite. About every third beat, it shudders like it's being tasered. So I move to my side a little to see what it will do next, and it goes really crazy—jumping around like a wild animal in a cage. This makes me nervous, and I sit up straight. Pretty soon my ticker is beating normally. I'm freaked out because I think it might suddenly stop if I'm not perfectly erect. Maybe I should see a heart specialist, I think. But then I figure I just won't lean back anymore.

A Dining Experience

He was a bold man who first ate an oyster.

Jonathan Swift

"You like the stew, boy?" asked the old man with missing teeth and a red knob for a nose seated across from us.

"It's good," I replied, gulping down a potato and carrot.

My dad eyed our fellow diner and nudged the side of my leg with his. That was his signal for me to be quiet.

"They don't give you seconds here like they do at the Sally, but this here tastes better than what they give you over there."

"Where's the Salvation Army you're talking about?" asked my father.

"Just about a mile up the road. You ain't staying here tonight?"

"Not sure," answered my father, and I knew we'd be hitting the road to the Sally after we ate. He didn't like the look of the shelter and the homeless men in it.

"They might give the boy another helping. Could ask. Never know," said the guy with the veiny schnoz.

"No, that's okay. I think he has all he can handle already. Thanks, though."

I bumped my dad's leg to let him know that wasn't true. I was still hungry. He bumped my leg back, and I gave him an angry sideways glance. He arched his eyebrow in return, which was another signal for me to shut up.

"Kids got hollow legs, you know. He's skinny but can probably out eat both of us."

When I lifted my spoon from the depths of the bowl, something in it caught my eye . . . because it seemed to be moving.

"Dad, what's this? I think it's a bug."

"Huh? What are you. . .?"

"Look, I think it's a fly. Is that what it is, Dad? Still alive, too," I said, holding the spoon near his face.

"No, it can't be," he replied, inspecting the object.

“Yeah, I bet it is,” commented the toothless man opposite us.

My father examined the spoon more closely and then advised me not to eat what was in it.

“Oh, go ahead, sonny. Just protein. They have bugs in the stew here all the time. Nothing to worry about. You probably ate a few already and didn’t even notice.”

Suddenly my stomach began to churn and what I’d just wolfed down gushed from my mouth.

“Now look what you gone and done, boy. Got puke all over my bread,” barked our tablemate, scraping my vomit from the crust near his bowl. “S’pose it won’t kill me, though . . .you being just a youngin.”

When the bum lifted it to his mouth, my father grabbed me by the arm and pulled me away from the bench we were sitting on.

“What are you doing, mister?” he growled.

“Eatin’ my dinner. What’s it look like?”

“C’mon, Mikey. Let’s get out of here. You’re disgusting, old man!”

"Excuse me, your lordship. Didn't know we were dining at the Ritz," he replied, running his dark tongue over his lips.

When we were outside of the mission, I threw up again.

"And you wanted seconds," snarled my father, handing me his dirty handkerchief.

Journal Entry

Yesterday I wrote about everything that happened to me at work. It was a day noteworthy for its interesting activities, challenging tasks, good meetings, and the arrival of our new DESTROYIT 4002 CROSS CUT LEVEL 4 paper shredder. Today I have nothing to report, because it's a holiday, and I didn't have to go into the office. So I guess there really isn't anything worth writing about.

Myles Shoots for Immortality

I'm getting used to the fact that
you find me incredibly forgettable.
Erica Cameron

Having recently hit retirement age, Myles felt that much—if not all—of his life had been spent in meaningless activities. Now, as he entered his senior years with a chronic ailment, he was determined to do one really exceptional thing that would be remembered after his passing . . . an act or deed that would make people sit up and take notice. The only problem he faced was an inability to think of any one thing that would lead to accomplishing his goal.

You can't run the Boston Marathon, climb Mt. Everest, explore Antarctica, reverse global warming, cure terminal cancer . . . Okay, dummy, c'mon, let's be sensible. Get back to reality . . . Stop thinking of stuff way beyond your skill level. So, let's see, you don't have a singing voice or the chops needed to act, dance, play an instrument, paint a portrait, or build anything. Crap! And you can hardly write a sentence without a mistake, so authoring a best-seller isn't going to happen. Double crap . . .! sulked Myles.

Weeks passed without the sexagenarian figuring out what he might do to permanently brand himself in people's minds. His desperation grew and he moped about his three-room flat frustrated with his lack of any viable idea. *There's nothing I can do to keep me in people's thoughts after I'm gone. I'll die and leave zero behind to attest to who I was or what I did.*

However, just when he felt he was doomed to exit the world without having accomplished a truly memorable feat, he came up with what he was certain would guarantee he'd never be forgotten. *This will do it*, he told himself. *I'll be permanently remembered for this.*

Early the next day, Myles set out to purchase what he needed to indelibly mark his time on Earth. He then gathered his few friends at his apartment. As they sat in his modestly furnished living room anticipating what Myles promised would be an enduring recollection for them, he pulled a gun from his pocket.

No one will forget me now, he thought, watching the horrified faces around him as he put the barrel to his temple and pulled the trigger.

Informed Viewers

A new study indicates that network television newscasts fail to give their audiences sufficient coverage of world events given the limited amount of time they devote to actual reporting. However, it did reveal that viewers are extremely well informed in matters concerning erectile dysfunction, dry eyes, bladder infections, arthritis, constipation, heartburn, psoriasis, memory loss, denture pain, back pain, and chronic gas.

The Pastor Vents at Stephen King's Wake

You thought there would be no consequences for all the dark and anguished narratives you scrawled—all those suffering characters doomed by your pen? But they won't just disappear to make way for your next macabre tale or to accommodate more of your stories about tortured souls. In the end, you will know of the debt you have accrued for what your savage imagination has wrought. Your inventions know that, too. On your deathbed you will be revisited by the boy you made a criminal, the mother whose child you deformed, the wife you turned into a monster, the schoolgirl you had ravaged, the continents you decimated. Your heinous portrayals will accompany you into eternal night. There will be no untroubled sleep for you. The madness you invoked will haunt your descendants as well, and they, too, will plead for mercy and curse your grim artistry.

Amen.

Varying Degrees of Perception

I park what is left of my wrecked car at the front of the auto body shop. When I enter the office, the young woman standing behind the counter asks if I've had an accident.

When You Fail to Consider the Logistics

"What do I do?" muttered Marvin, contemplating the challenge of climbing two flights of steep stairs to get to his work area as his legs became less and less reliable. *At 81, I shouldn't be in this old house*, he told himself and reviewed the options for remaining in the place he'd occupied for 43 years. *Could set up my work area down here on the first floor. There's enough room. Screw what it looks like. Nobody visits me anymore since Clare died anyway. Yeah, that's what I'll do . . . but how do I get the 21 foot sailboat I've been building downstairs?*

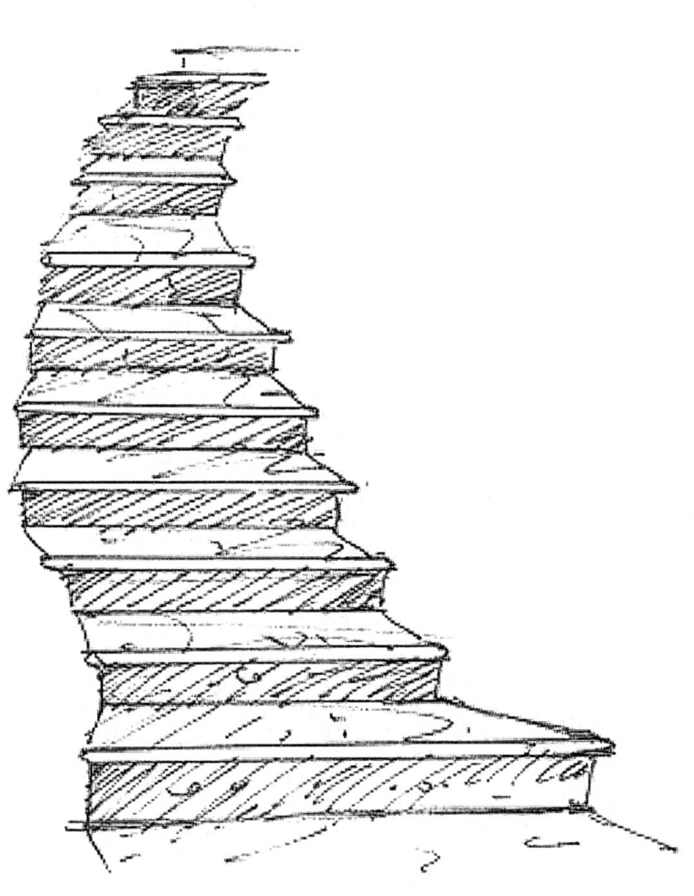

A Record Effect

My cousin, Danny, bought the Beatles' *Magical Mystery Tour* album as soon as it arrived in the record store and disappeared into his room for six months. When he emerged, he displayed an aberrant fear of polar bears and an immense craving for benthic invertebrates.

Upgrade

The three-star hotel featured some nice amenities, but one in particular was quite extraordinary. For an additional ten dollars, guests could rent a room that offered a human teleporter able to beam them to a 4-star hotel.

Enough, Already!

A small wooden cross stood at the side of the busy highway where Sharon had lost her life. Two weeks after it was erected, her close friend, Toni, stopped to put a flower on it and was struck by a passing car. Another cross was placed next to Sharon's, and a month later a cousin of Toni's, Karen, arrived to pay tribute to her and was crushed by an 18-wheeler. Along with Sharon and Toni's crosses, a third was erected for Karen. Following the harsh winter, the memorials were in ill repair, so all three mothers of the deceased young women arrived to restore the makeshift site. As fate would have it . . .

Blowin' in the Wind

Bought me a Hohner Blue Midnight mouth harp to begin makin' music. Somethin' I been planin' to do for ages. Once started learnin' the thing, then forgot about it. Was 30 years back, and what I learned then is long gone. Always promised myself I would pickup on an instrument before I died, and that date is gettin' closer. Seventy-eight ain't a kid, so it's now or never.

*

Been intendin' to get going on the Hohner sooner than later. Settin' there on the coffee table in front of me while I watch the television, read the newspaper, and look out the window at the snow pilin', but still ain't start learnin' it. Gonna though . . . you betcha'. Shameful if'n I don't after spendin' good money on it and promisin' myself I would learn it 'afore I croak. Maybe start tomorrow. Yep, gotta' do it.

*

There's dust on that damn harmonica 'cause I ain't done nothin' with it. Surely bothers me I ain't start workin' it to make tunes. Just ain't got 'round to it 'cause other stuff keepin' me from it. Them lessons came with it need concentratin', too, and I ain't been in no concentratin' mood lately. I'll get to it, 'cause it ain't like me not to do somethin' when I say I will.

*

That Hohner starin' at me like I done wrong by it, and maybe I have. 'Spose to be blown but ain't got the wind in me to do it 'cause of that COPD stuff. Ain't my fault so shouldn't feel I done a crime on it. Shoot, I *do*, though. Best I just put it away for the time bein.' Can't do nothin' by it now anyways.

Lateral Movement

Everything seemed out of kilter to Carson as he drove to the gas station. The planet felt out of plumb . . . like a meteor had bumped into it causing everything to lean hard in one direction. He wasn't sure what was happening but believed it did not bode well. He feared he may have had a stroke or that a brain tumor was causing his loss of equilibrium. While his car was receiving a tune up, his anxiety mounted. *This has got to be something bad. I've never had anything like it before. Better see the doctor right away before I fall over. I'm out of whack.* Before he could finish dialing his primary care physician, the mechanic emerged. "Sir, you really need a front end alignment. Must feel like you're being pulled off the road."

You Never Know What You'll Get with a Shelter Dog

To ease her loneliness, recently widowed Marge Segal adopted a dog. It was a nine month-old Border Collie mix, and it was very sweet and smart. She didn't know how smart until one morning it made her a low-fat Caramel Brulée Latte.

Hard to Read

Three women poets were the first to present their work at the Elm Street Consortium for the Arts. All were young, attractive, and gifted orators. The first wrote of giving birth and the joy of transcendent love. The second had elegantly composed lyrics relating to a magical place her mother took her when she was a child. The third poetess spoke of her transformational experience following a domestic mishap and how it gave her strength she did not know she possessed. Warm and appreciative applause followed each of their recitations. There was a palpable change in mood among those in attendance when the only man on the schedule read his dark stanzas with affecting emphasis. Not one of his verses contained the words birth, joy, love, magical, or child. Instead kill, bomb, war, rape, and destroy suffused his narratives. A tentative silence followed his reading and then the audience sprang to its feet and cheered wildly.

Do You Do This, Too?

In your fantasies of tragedies, you always have your loved ones surviving.

Careful What You Ask

Barry fantasized his wife having passionate sex with her former boyfriend. It both aroused and disturbed him. It was, however, the fastest way for him to get off, so he conjured the images frequently.

Eventually, they took their toll on his marriage because he developed resentment for his spouse. While he realized it was stupid to be jealous over something that occurred before he was even on the scene, it still ate at him.

"What's the matter, honey? You seem so distant lately," observed his wife.

For a long time, Barry said nothing about what was actually bothering him, and then the need to broach the subject overtook him.

"You had great sex with the guy before me, right?" he ventured.

"Which one are you talking about?" she replied.

Why Assistant Fiction Editors Get Assaulted

"I don't see much texture or imagination here. Mostly what you've written is mundane description that really doesn't lead anywhere. You might consider shifting your efforts to penning corporate copy. I think it may better suit your particular skill set."

No Pressure Here

Writer Norman Corwin is on a train bound for Los Angeles in 1941. Along the way he receives an urgent message from Washington that he is to immediately pen a radio play designed to rally the spirit and resolve of the nation as it faces potential obliteration.

When Life's Load Becomes Too Much

Ralph developed a membrane over the opening of his anus, which eventually kept him from excreting. Toxins built up in his body, poisoning his organs and causing a fatal heart arrhythmia. His putrefied, bloated, and blistering corpse was found slumped against the tank of the commode. On the floor next to him was a note revealing the depth of Ralph's despair:

I just don't give a shit anymore . . . and haven't for a very long time.

One of the attending medics, an English major, appreciated what he felt was the missive's ironic humor.

Desperate

When you look at images of Texas panhandle towns online, they all look the same. In fact, if you key in Dalhart or Hereford or Muleshoe, you may think they're using the same photograph. Now, I don't know why they'd be doing that, because that picture shows a dusty, drab, windblown main street with vacant storefronts. It's not something you'd think they'd post on Google, but maybe it's the best they can do.

Howard Has a Troubling Experience with His Senses

Something clicked in his head, and his world was thrown out of kilter. Now it seemed as if he were living under water . . . everything seemed muddled. For days his condition persisted until he decided to see his doctor. On his way to his appointment, fate intervened. Only a block away, he sneezed hard and suddenly all returned to normal—his hearing cleared. He was about to turn around and return home when something entered his right eye forcing him to pull to the side of the road. It felt like his cornea had been scratched. After a failed attempt to address it, he continued on to his appointment. He informed his doctor that while his ear trouble had resolved itself he now had an issue with his eye. To his relief, the doctor took care of it and sent him on his way. When he pulled into his driveway, he experienced a sudden terrible tingling in his nose that prompted him to thrust his fingers into both nostrils. Deep inside he could feel something furry moving about. "Oh my, God!" he yelped and pulled at whatever it was. Within seconds, he'd extracted the kitten that had disappeared while he'd slept next to it. *Aha*, thought Howard, *that's what all this was about.*

Tuscaloosa, Alabama, 1938

She looked out the window from the back of the bus at all the white folks going about their lives and wished she had one, too.

What They See

When we were little, my sister became excited when a brilliant shaft of light shone through an opening in a cloud and touched down in a field in front of us. "It's God!" she declared, looking on in utter wonderment. Sixty years later when I took her for a walk in the garden of the nursing home for Alzheimer patients, she made the same joyous declaration when God made another appearance.

Parents Be Talking Bullshit

Her father kept reminding her of the importance of keeping her job at the Waffle House.

"But Dad, I'd make more from unemployment compensation than I do busing dishes and cleaning tables," she responded.

"Perhaps," he countered, "but you wouldn't have your pride."

A Colorful Allegory

Explorer Louis Pantone found escape in his dreams wherein all living beings were of one color and hatred did not exist. Unfortunately, his conscious world was very different from his dream world—mired as it was in rampant discrimination and hostility between contrasting skin tones. His particular hue—Greentones—was the largest, comprising 37 percent of the world's population. Next were the Taupetones at 16 percent. The Fuchsiatones, Pucetones, Lavendertones, Graytones, Bluetones, Indigotones, Limetones, Orangetones, Yellowtones, and Purpletones followed in that order. Nobody wished to be among the latter four tints, which were classified as Lowtones. Then Pantone and his team discovered cognitive beings in a jungle of an uncharted archipelago. They were of a hitherto unknown shade. While some embraced them, most did not—considering them unsightly outliers. Consequently, the presence of the Blacktones resulted in the elevation of the Limetones, allowing that class of hues to more fully enjoy the benefits afforded the dominant colors.

If Only Things Were This Way

Liver and onions was on the diner menu for 99 cents. Buck had only 87 cents, so he calculated what he should not eat, since he lacked the full cost of the meal. He pushed a small slice of liver and a piece of onion to the side of his plate and quickly devoured the rest, savoring every bite. When it came time to pay his bill, he handed over what he figured he owed. "Thank you, sir," said the cashier, "I hope you enjoyed your food."

Why It Was Ill-Advised to Go Outside

A security camera revealed a preternaturally large figure skulking about the parking garage. To those catching a glimpse of it on the monitor, it appeared inhuman—bearlike but with giant silver barbs jetting out in several directions from its body. A horrible roar startled employees moving down the hall that led to the building's exit. It was 5 o'clock and time to go home.

Literary Investigation

The question that loomed large in the minds of many in the Academy was what had David Foster Wallace done to guarantee the wellbeing of his beloved dogs as he prepared to commit suicide? After extensive research, noted scholar Dr. Larry Collette concluded that the acclaimed author likely figured that whoever discovered his body would feed Werner and Bella.

Photo Noir

A body slumps in the Hudson convertible sedan. Its bloodied head hangs from the window. Cops are standing around waiting for the coroner to arrive. Already on the scene is Weegee, the ubiquitous press photographer. This is the second killing he's shot since midnight. He hopes he'll get in a couple more black-and-whites of low-life before the night is over. *It's been a slow one*, he thinks.

A Woman Alone

Sybil remained in her booth at the Club Danube after finishing her third Sloe Gin Fuzz. *One more Chesterfield*, she thought, *and then if he doesn't come back, I'll leave.* The ballroom was emptying out and Sybil felt conspicuously forsaken. *What a bastard he was to leave me like this. He seemed so nice, too. Men are just . . . I shouldn't have told him my real age.* Sybil collected her purse and wrap and made her way to the door. As she was about to exit the nightspot, a voice called her name. It was the man who'd abandoned her. "Sorry, love, I was in the little boy's room all this time with the worst case of diarrhea you could imagine." Sybil couldn't wait to get back to his apartment.

Selected Books from PalmArtPress

John Berger / Liane Birnberg
garden on my cheek
ISBN: 978-3-941524-77-4
60 Pages, Poetry/Art, Softcover/flaps, English

Carmen-Francesca Banciu
Berlin Is My Paris- *Stories from the Capital*
ISBN: 978-3-941524-66-8 *
204 Pages, English

Michael Lederer
In the Widdle Wat of Time
ISBN: 978-3-941524-70-5 *
150 Pages, poetry and very short stories, Hardcover, English

Dorothea Flechsig
NightSwim
ISBN: 978-3-941524-72-9
60 Pages, Poetry, Hardcover, English/German

Manfred Giesler
The Yellow Wallpaper *Ein Monologue*
ISBN: 978-3-941524-75-0 *
68 Pages, Theatre, open-thread cover, English/German

Carmen-Francesca Banciu
Mother's Day - *Song of a Sad Mother*
ISBN: 978-3-941524-47-7 *
244 Pages, English

Alexander de Cadenet
Afterbirth - *Poems & Inversions*
ISBN: 978-3-941524-59-0
64Pages, Poetry/Art, Softcover/flaps, English

Jörg Rubbert
Paris-New York-Berlin - *Streetphotography 1978 - 2010*
ISBN: 978-3-941524-58-3
260 Pages, Photo Retrospective, Softcover/flaps, English/German

Runhild Wirth
Come Here, I Want to Ruin You!
Palast der Republik - Analysis of Dissolution
ISBN: 978-3-941524-52-1
120 Pages, Poetry/Art, Hardcover, English/German

Wolfgang Nieblich
Distant Yet so Near or **The Currywurst**
ISBN: 978-3-941524-49-1 (EN) *
64 Pages, 18 Coloured Fotos, Engliish

Michael Lederer
The Great Game - ***Berlin-Warschau Express and Other Stories***
ISBN: 978-3-941524-12-5 (EN) *
242 Pages, 18 Short Stories, Softcover, English

Michael Lederer
Nothing Lasts Forever Anymore
ISBN: 978-3-941524-33-0 (EN) *
124 Pages, Novel, Softcover, English

Maria Reinecke
La Rambla - *Barcelona Story*
ISBN: 978-3-941524-20-0 (EN) *
91 Pages, Short Story, English

Maria Reinecke
LIVING IN BETWEEN
ISBN: 978-3-941524-22-4 (EN) *
180 Pages, Novel, Softcover, English

* Also available as E-Book